"The plot moves effortlessly from a young man's trauma-filled youth to his finding the right vocation and the right partner. That may sound boring, but I became easily captured by the main character and was rooting for him all the way. Mr. Sisti is equally self-assured when writing the details of an Adirondack wilderness or the advertising game in New York City. As the characters develop, the author's sense of humor peeks through in a delightful way. And, as a psychologist, I enjoy reading how two emotionally intelligent though imperfect adults combine their lives to become a formidable team battling against very difficult work experiences and very difficult other people. I found myself at the end of this book wanting to reach for the next book in this series so that I could continue to have these characters in my life."

—**Deborah Donaldson**, Author, Psychologist

"*On the Brink* is an apt title for the drama of this book. It is the breath-holding saga of Dave Powers, who struggles for survival in business and love. More than that, it is a snapshot of real life where there is only one direction of travel: forward. For many readers, it will be an agonizing reminder of the agony most of us have faced in toxic work environments where politics and nepotism had a greater role than competence. This is a saga of the most turbulent profession: advertising. The work is more than one of literature; it is an in-the-weeds look at keeping one's sanity in a world where alcoholism, exploitation of women, and the 'one mistake and you are gone' culture are a reality. The book is a work of triumph over human adversity and is not for the literary fainthearted."

—**Steve Levi**, Alaskan Historian, Author of Eighty Books

"Michael A. Sisti invites the reader into the life of Dave Powers, from a boyhood riddled with tragedy to a young man who learns to cope using his talent for business. However, success is fraught with trials and tribulations. The bright side is he finds love, but even that takes an unexpected turn. *On the Brink* is a poignant story interlaced with equal parts of harsh reality and subtle humor."—**J. Schlenker**, Author

"Sisti has done it again—proven himself to be proficient in multiple genres of writing. While he is perhaps best known for his humorous writings and his business guides, this work demonstrates his ability to craft a compelling dramatic story. *On the Brink* paints a picture of a young man who is beaten down by tragedy and bad luck yet pulls himself up by his own merits to achieve success and a lasting love. Reading this account of the young life of Dave Powers makes me want to go back to reread his later adventures in Executive Crumple Zone and Executive Bone Yard. Well done, Michael."

—**Rosalie J. Regni**, Fashion Executive, Fashion Professor, Virginia Commonwealth University, Retired

"Mr. Sisti serves up a potent cocktail of high-stakes tension and romance as we follow our hero through his journey of fierce struggle from adolescence to adulthood—from the street to the office—surviving crippling adversity. Dave Powers is an entrepreneurial warrior, and this page-turner does what every novel should do: reaffirm the joy of life."

—**Nick DeSimone**, Award-Winning Playwright and Filmmaker

"*On the Brink* pulls you in quickly with surprising twists and turns. The writing, especially the dialogue, is exceptional. I highly recommend indulging in this fantastic story, written by an author who is a master of his craft."

—**Lizzy Wright**, Author

"Captivating from the get-go, it's such an easy, thrilling, yet humorous read. Your mouth will hit the floor at least three times with Sisti's imagination, sprinkled with truths, which makes it difficult to put *On the Brink* down. This book is perfect for the entertainment of reading but also for important lessons learned about business, disappointment, perseverance, and love."

—**Ann B**, Country Club Membership Director

"*On the Brink* had me hooked from the prologue to the end! The story follows the main character, Dave Powers', journey through a life filled with tragedy, success, failure, and love as Dave strives to succeed in the competitive world of advertising. Each turn of events, from the mystery surrounding his mother's murder to the strange circumstances that lead Dave to pursue a career in advertising, kept me engaged in the story and wanting more. On the Brink is definitely one of Sisti's best!"

—**Joanne Bilotta,** Principal and Co-founder, Exigent Key

"*On the Brink* is a fast-reading book about business and life. It follows the life of Dave, who learns how to bounce back from personal tragedies, successfully reinventing himself each time. We know that life isn't one smooth ride, but we all have ups and downs to handle. For anyone interested in what really happens in business and how to be successful, especially as an entrepreneur, this is a must-read. You won't want to put it down."

—**Howard H. Prager,** Author of *Make Someone's Day: Becoming a Memorable Leader in Work and Life*

"An exciting and informative novel for readers young and old. An eleven-year-old boy becomes a successful entrepreneur selling fireworks, but real, life-threatening fireworks are yet to come. I highly recommend this coming-of-age story about the deadly pitfalls in life."

—**Susan Klaus,** Award-Winning Author of Fantasies and Thrillers

"*On the Brink* is an adventurous exploration of entrepreneurial determination, painful losses, and navigating a world filled with evil. Based on a true story, it's an eye-opening read for aspiring young people and the mentors who help them become productive adults."

—**B. Lynn Goodwin,** Author of *Talent and Never Too Late: From Wannabe to Wife at 62*, Owner, Writer Advice

"Dave Powers is in his office at night when he hears trucks pulling up and angry men beating on his door and yelling for him to come out. . . . He manages to escape, not knowing what's going on or how he's going to get out of this. Author Mike Sisti has a way of engaging his readers from page one, and *On the Brink* is no exception, the first in a series of five adventures of Dave Powers; his successes and mistakes in business and his attempts at romance are suspenseful beyond the ordinary. Grab on for the first one, *On the Brink*!"

—**Eleanor McCallie Cooper,** Author *Dragonfly Dreams*

"In his new novel, *On the Brink*, Michael Sisti gives his readers a character anyone can find common ground with. His raging successes coupled with devastating nadirs come with a fast-paced storytelling style that keeps the pages turning. Dave Powers is someone we cheer for, groan with, and ultimately become friends with as he grows in the hectic business world of New York. A recommended read for everyone, it especially resonates with young readers wanting to find what their future may hold. It is an engaging story about life as we live it every day, providing encouragement in disaster and fulfillment in the simple pleasures we should not take for granted."

—**Brandon Currence,** Author of *Looking for
the Seams and The Maine Consecration*

"5 STARS! Star one: intriguing and compelling storyline. Star two: well-developed characters. Star three: vivid scene descriptions. Star four: believable (and surprising) twists and reveals. Start five: clear and critical backstory. And you are left wanting more! I can easily imagine *On the Brink* as a string of books featuring Dave Powers' ongoing journey and a made-for-TV series! Bravo, Mr. Sisti. Well done!"

—**Michael H. Samuelson,** Author of *Beyond Survival:
Living a Life of Thrival*

On the Brink

by Michael A. Sisti

ISBN 979-8-88824-129-5

Published by

 köehlerbooks™

3705 Shore Drive
Virginia Beach, VA 23455
800-435-4811

ON THE BRINK

BOOK ONE OF A FIVE BOOK SERIES

Chaos and Mayhem at the Office

MICHAEL A. SISTI

VIRGINIA BEACH
CAPE CHARLES

This book is dedicated to
the amazing woman who shared
most of the experiences described in this book,
Sara O. Sisti

PROLOGUE

Returning home about 9 p.m., he looked out the window and saw that a light was on in his office. He walked across the gravel drive and into the small building that housed his business. There was a note on the desk left by his warehouse assistant. As he sat reading it, the sound of cars and trucks coming up his mile-long driveway got his attention. He looked out and saw the headlights of dozens of vehicles and realized something was wrong. He almost never had visitors, especially at night. Quickly putting out the lights, he waited in the dark office watching the ominous caravan approach.

An unruly gang of angry men jumped out of their trucks and ran to the cabin's front door, banging on it and yelling. One screamed over them, "Come out, you murdering bastard!"

He recognized the men from the bar he had just left. They were all shouting and cursing, but he couldn't understand why.

"Surround the house. Don't let him get away."

"Burn the fucking place down."

"He don't belong here."

Then someone threw a rock through his front window, followed by a gas can. In seconds his cabin was ablaze with the men cheering.

"Burn, you prick!"

"You deserve to die in hell!"

The incensed crowd, lubricated with beer and whiskey shots, were out of control. They started smashing the other windows and torching everything. He knew he was in mortal danger but had no idea what was happening. He quietly left through the back door of the building and ran down the driveway. Halfway to Rt. 28, he turned and saw the cabin, warehouse, and his Jeep all in a roaring inferno.

Once on the highway, he continued running towards town, jumping into the trees whenever a car passed. A side road brought him around the inhabited area of the town and back onto the highway.

Once past the town, he stepped into the woods and sat on a rock. There he labored to catch his breath as he tried to figure out what was happening to him. *Why are they trying to kill me? It doesn't make sense. I have to get as far away from here as I can.*

When he recovered his stamina, he continued running away from town down Rt. 28, not knowing where to go.

PART I

The Formative Years—On Steroids

CHAPTER 1

The Schoolyard

THE NOISY ENERGY of 250 kids congregating in the schoolyard before class could be felt for blocks. It urged Dave Powell to hurry there to greet his pals. Dave was 11 and in sixth grade. He arrived dressed like the other boys in his school uniform of blue slacks, white dress shirt, and patterned school tie. He was of average height and build with wavy brown hair to match his dark brown eyes. He was always upbeat and wore a perpetual smile as his eyes and ears searched for the humor in everything around him.

Gifted with exceptional intelligence and a take-charge attitude, he achieved the highest grades of any of the boys in his class with almost no effort. This frustrated the nuns who saw even more potential in him.

His best friend George Cranmer came up to him on this Friday morning, May 1, 1953. George was taller than Dave, with blonde hair, blue eyes, and a deceptively angelic look about him. "Dave, it's May, the start of firecracker season. Tomorrow morning we're all going to Chinatown to buy some cherry bombs and stuff."

"Oh, shit. I forgot. Yeah, I'm in. Who's going with us?"

"Petey, Vinnie, and Frederick."

"Why can't we call him Freddie? Why do we have to use his whole name?"

"You know why. It's his bitchy mother. No nicknames for her perfect son."

The school bell rang and everyone got in their class lines, according to height. Sister Mary Grouch, as the kids referred to her, sternly began calling in the classes, starting with first grade.

Getting to his desk, Dave sat right down and took out his unfinished homework. He quickly completed the math questions while the class was getting settled. He detested homework. He considered it a failure on the part of the teachers, convinced they could complete their lessons between 9 a.m. and 3 p.m. That was more than enough time taken out of his busy day.

He also suspected the nuns contrived the idea of homework to occupy their students' minds so they wouldn't have any impure thoughts after school. He disliked the nuns, wearing their black habits, oversize rosary beads on their rope belts, and constantly clutching the large crucifix around their necks. Adding to the overkill, he didn't appreciate their devotion to the church and their mission to move all the children closer to God. He had more important things to do, like basketball and swimming. And tomorrow they were going to Chinatown!

CHAPTER 2

Explosive Inflation

THE NEXT MORNING, Dave, wearing his Lee jeans and a tee shirt, left the house on his way to the subway station. He lived on the east side of Manhattan in the east-fifties. It was an upper-income neighborhood of mostly attached brownstones with a flight of concrete steps leading up to each front door landing.

As he crossed the street, Mrs. Grabenstetter was at her window. Seeing him, she opened the window and said, "Good morning, David. Are you going to the grocery store?"

"Not now. I'm meeting my friends and we're going to Chinatown to buy some firecrackers. I can go to the store for you later."

Smiling at him, she said, "Okay. Stop by when you have time."

Dave pumped his fist as he ran down the street. *This is great. She always gives me a nice tip. Now I can use all my allowance for the firecrackers and save the tip money for the rest of the week.*

He liked Mrs. Grabenstetter. She wasn't a crank like some of the other nosy people on the street, and she always tipped him when he ran errands for her. He knew she lived alone and was retired from the Air Force, but she never told him how her husband died. Although her face was smooth, he considered her old because she was bent over and had gray hair. She also didn't have a job like his mom and dad.

The five boys gathered at the 59th Street subway entrance, went down to the platform with its grimy white tiled walls, and took the train downtown to Grand Street. From there, they walked to Mott Street and into Chinatown. It was completely different from Little Italy, only one block away. All the store signs were both in English and Chinese. The sidewalks were crowded with traditionally-dressed Asians. It was like being in another country.

The boys soon encountered some young Chinese men who offered to sell them fireworks. They were disappointed to learn that packs of firecrackers had increased to 25 cents, and ashcans and cherry bombs were also a quarter each. The year before those items were selling for ten to 15 cents each.

Dave asked one of the street vendors if he could get the big stuff.

"How big you want?" came the reply. "I got helicopters and roman candles, but no rockets."

Disappointed, Dave asked, "How much are the helicopters?"

"Helicopters $2.00, roman candles, same."

The boys spent about a dollar or two each for firecrackers and cherry bombs and then headed back to the subway station.

On the way home, George sat next to Dave and expressed his disappointment. "Can you believe the prices? They go up every year. This really sucks."

"Well, I'm not going back there just to get ripped off again. I saw an ad in one of the comic books. It's from a fireworks company in Ohio offering the big stuff for really low prices. I just have to figure out how to get them delivered. The city is so strict, you can't even buy sparklers anywhere."

"Forget it, Dave. I looked into it last year. You have to have a $50 order before they will ship you anything. But if you ordered that much, they send it by Railway Express. I ain't got that kind of money, do you?"

"No, of course not. But how about this? I'm gonna get their price list and take orders from everyone in our class. I'll come up with the fifty bucks. You in?"

"Listen to yourself. It's not like the Chinese selling packs of firecrackers in Chinatown. The cops look the other way down there. You start selling fireworks in our neighborhood and they will put your ass in jail."

"Bullshit! How are they gonna catch us? They don't have time for kids in Catholic school." Getting excited about the idea, he added, "Think about it, Georgie boy. We could make some money and have a bunch of serious rockets to bring to Boy Scout camp in July. I'm doing it."

Becoming convinced by Dave's enthusiasm, George said, "Yeah, you're right. We'd be hot shit at Ten Mile River when we show up with rockets. Let's go for it. How can we lose?"

CHAPTER 3

Launching the Caper

THE 9 A.M. CHILDREN'S MASS on Sundays was like being in prison. All the kids sat in the pews by class with their teacher behind them to make sure they didn't talk. Although Dave had been an altar boy, he hated this strict ritual each week. When he got home from the Mass that morning, his parents Brad and Virginia were getting ready to go to the later service. Brad, who had a master's degree in accounting, worked for IBM in White Plains. Virginia was a psychiatrist, practicing from their home office. They had met at NYU while studying for their degrees.

Brad was six feet tall, 200 pounds with straight dirty blond hair, mixed with a little gray. His dark brown eyes were framed with horned-rim glasses, and he had a distinguished but serious look about him. He wore what he referred to as his IBM uniform, a navy-blue suit with a white shirt and red tie.

Virginia, by contrast, was five-foot-four with a trim figure and had a wardrobe that filled two closets. She wore a deep red skirt suit with a gray silk blouse. Her hair was black with thin matching eyebrows and smooth white skin. A beautiful oval face framed her large hazel eyes and full red lips.

As soon as his parents left for church, Dave went into their home office in the ground floor basement to type a letter to the fireworks company. The office served primarily as Virginia's practice location where she met with her patients. Table lamps warmly lit the room's mahogany desk and leather visitor's chair. Along the side wall was a plush couch with a side table. A row of file cabinets lined the back wall along with Virginia's framed degrees. Although it was an office that both parents used, the two large front windows and the homey décor gave the setting an inviting comfortable feel, designed to relax her patients.

As an IBM executive, Brad had access to the company's latest electric typewriter which had a type correction feature. It still took Dave three tries to type an office-quality note to the firm, requesting their price list. He then carefully removed the mistyped letters and put them in his schoolbag to throw away the next day.

When he was finished, he got his basketball and went into the unfinished storage area in the rear of the basement. He switched off the light, leaving him in near total darkness, and began dribbling his basketball. He practiced without being able to see the ball, spinning around and switching hands as he dribbled the ball between his legs and around his back. He did this exercise every day and it enabled him to compete at basketball with older kids who were much taller than him.

A week after mailing the letter, Dave began checking the trash basket in the office every day as soon as he got home from school. He knew his mother always opened the mail in the office, discarding the envelopes and junk mail. A few days later, he was rewarded. A color catalog from Ohio Fireworks was laying in the bin among the clutter.

Scanning the eight-page brochure, Dave gushed with excitement. He raced over to George's house. Together, they began fantasizing about the exotic fireworks they wanted to buy for themselves. When they reviewed the pricing, they realized that they could sell all the basic products for twice what they cost and still undercut Chinatown. It would give them a huge profit.

Dave started making a list of the most popular items and put a selling price next to each one. George copied the list for his own use.

The next morning, they got to the schoolyard early and they each approached boys congregating in small groups. As soon as the kids heard the prices, they began ordering, promising to pay as soon as they got their allowance.

Within ten minutes there was a huge flock around each of them, with everyone scrambling to place an order. But then, Dave looked up and saw one of the sisters in her black and white habit approaching the group to see about the commotion. Using slang and the Pig Latin phrase, *ixnay*, meaning *nix* as a warning, he said, "Ixnay, penguin sighting." He then walked away from the crowd.

With her headpiece billowing, she corralled the group, asking the boys what was going on. One of them answered, "We're just trading baseball cards." Since no cards were in anyone's hands, she exhaled in frustration, knowing they were lying.

At about 5 p.m., Dave was in his room copying orders from his notes on scraps of paper to a notebook. He hadn't planned on the crush of kids wanting to place orders and wasn't well prepared. The doorbell rang, and his mother called up to him that there were some boys at the front door to see him.

When Dave saw that they were high school boys, he went to the outside landing, closing the door behind him. One of the boys said to him, "Hey, you're Dave, right? We heard you're selling firecrackers and stuff real cheap. We want to buy some."

Dave became alarmed. He couldn't have his parents knowing he was dealing in illegal fireworks. They would ground him, and maybe even cancel his trip to Boy Scout camp.

He nodded toward the door, waved his hand in a nervous gesture, and said, "Look, I can't talk here. Meet me after school tomorrow at the park by Sutton Place."

"You got it, Dave. We'll be there."

When Dave came back into the house, his mother asked, "Who were those boys? They look like high school boys. What do they want with you?"

"Yeah, I know them from the playground. They asked me to join a basketball team with them on Saturdays. They think I'm pretty good."

At the end of class the next day, Dave's teacher asked to have a word with him about his homework. This caused him to get to the park a few minutes late.

When he arrived, there were over thirty boys waiting for him. Trying to hide his anxiety and fear, he strutted over to the group. They all crowded around him trying to give him their orders. They were each spending about five dollars, as many of them had part-time jobs.

He couldn't believe how easy this was. At the same time, it made him tense. He kept looking around, expecting a cop to show up and arrest him.

He left the park as soon as all the orders were placed and ran all the way to George's house. Together, they counted the orders, which were now approaching $300.

Another group of boys from the high school showed up at his house the next day. Dave was in a near-panic mode, as he knew his mother was going to grill him on these older boys coming to the house. He told them to let everyone know they were not to come to his house. He would be at the park every day after school for the next week. Back inside, his mother was now suspicious of him and asked who they were.

Lying again, he averted his eyes and said, "The kids are forming a league, and we're going to play teams from other neighborhoods. It's going to be fun."

Not satisfied with his answer, she warned him, "I'm not sure what you're up to, but you better not get into trouble, you hear me?"

"Mom, it's okay. I'm as good as the big kids. You should see my jump shot." Before she could ask more questions, he rushed up to his room. *She's not convinced.*

On Saturday morning, Dave had breakfast and left to go play

basketball up at the schoolyard. The basketball courts were three blocks from his house, and his routine was to run the entire way, practicing dribbling around his back, and between his legs, as he raced along. It was a tough regimen, but he felt it made him a better player. *Maybe if mom saw me play, she would believe my story about playing against high school kids.*

CHAPTER 4

Anxiety by the Truckload

As MAY CAME to an end, George and Dave stopped taking orders and made a list of the items and quantities to purchase from Ohio Fireworks. Dave typed the list and they walked to the Western Union office, got a money order, and sent out their fireworks order.

On the way back, they were giddy. Dave said, "Let's stop at the soda fountain in Woolworths and treat ourselves to chocolate egg creams. We can pay for it out of our profit."

They had sold over $500 worth of merchandise and had a profit of more than $200 after they each ordered a dozen rockets, helicopters, and mortars for their own use at Ten Mile River camp.

Two weeks later, the call came to George's house from Railway Express that there were four boxes to be picked up. George had volunteered to use his phone number since his parents both worked and he could check the phone during the day.

Dave had a Radio Flyer wagon in the shed behind his house. He used it for carting home groceries for shoppers at the supermarket. The two boys walked the 15 long avenues to the west side to pick up the order.

When the clerk brought the boxes out, they went from excitement to fear. In bright red letters, the boxes were marked, "Danger! Fireworks! Keep Away from Fire and Flame."

Not expecting the warning signage, George said, "I didn't think to bring a blanket to cover the boxes."

Out on the street, they frantically discussed how they were going to get the boxes home without being spotted by a police car. Dave suggested, "George, you pull the wagon, and I'll walk on the street side of the wagon to try to hide the boxes as best I can."

The biggest problem was crossing all the wide avenues, and they had to navigate nine of them to get back home. They started out strolling casually, with Dave hunched over the boxes. This lasted about a block, and then they found themselves nearly running and sweating with fear. The harrowing hour-long walk was one of the most frightening experiences of their young lives.

At one point, George said, "Ixnay, cop car coming down the street."

"Oh, shit. Don't look at it." The car passed without incident. All told, three police cars passed them along the route, but the patrolmen never took notice of the two terrified young boys or their contraband.

Finally, relieved and dripping with perspiration, they got to George's house and moved the boxes into his basement. By then they couldn't believe they hadn't been arrested. They began separating the merchandise for each order. The firecrackers, which most of the boys ordered, came wrapped in bundles of 144 packs. The ashcans and cherry bombs were packed seventy-two to a box.

As they prepared to put together each of the scores of individual orders, they realized that they had no provision to pack them. Dave said, "Wait here, I can get bags."

He ran to the neighborhood grocery store where he did all the quick-stop shopping for his mother, Mrs. Grabenstetter, and a couple of other neighbors. He was in the store nearly every day and knew the owner. He asked to buy 100 small paper bags. The owner asked why he needed so many, and Dave answered, "We're working on a school project."

When told they would cost two cents each, Dave handed him

two dollars, took the bags, and ran back to George's house. As they were filling the bags and putting names on them, they soon realized they did not have enough firecrackers and cherry bombs to fill all the orders. It was nearly dinner time, and Dave had to go home for supper. George offered to review all the orders and inventory to see where the error occurred.

Later that evening, George called Dave, "We didn't buy enough stuff to cover all the orders, and it's too late to order more."

On the verge of panic, Dave said, "Let's say we cut back each order and tell everyone there was a price increase."

"That's a good idea. If we do that, then we get to keep the profit we made. But do you think the kids are going to be mad?"

Still struggling with the decision, Dave said, "I'm more worried about the high school kids. If they find out, they'll beat the hell out of us. Let's give them a little more than the kids in our school."

They agreed to meet at George's the next day and repack all the orders.

After hanging up, Dave went to his room, unaware that his father had overheard the entire phone conversation.

CHAPTER 5

Lessons Learned

THE NEXT MORNING, just before class, George set off a cherry bomb. Having the same effect as the chimes on a Good Humor Ice Cream truck, all the kids ran over to where he was standing.

"Did the fireworks get here?" one of them asked.

Before he could answer, an angry nun came over and demanded, "Who set off that firecracker?"

Without answering, everyone scattered and the sister shouted, "Don't you walk away from me. I want to know who has firecrackers."

The bell rang, and everyone rushed to their lines and walked into class, but for the rest of the day there was a buzz among the kids that the fireworks had arrived. When asked during the day, Dave and George told their friends that the orders would be ready the next day.

After class, the two entrepreneurs raced to George's to repack the bags. When they finished, each order was short a couple of packs of firecrackers and cherry bombs. They assumed that everyone would be so excited about getting their stash, that they wouldn't count the contents. They decided they would explain the fictitious price increase only if questioned.

As expected, dozens of kids started showing up at George's the next day after school to pick up their loot. As they handed out the bags, Dave warned them, "Don't shoot off any near George's house. We don't want the cops turning up here."

That night after dinner, Dave's doorbell started ringing, as some of the kids began showing up at his house. They wanted to know why their orders were short. As he answered the door, he looked back inside to see if his parents were nearby. He nervously closed the door and stepped outside to explain the price increase, but they weren't happy about it. Looking down, Dave apologized, saying, "There was nothing we could do. We didn't want to cancel the order. And besides, it's still a lot cheaper than Chinatown." The boys left, but they weren't satisfied.

A while later, George called with more bad news. "Dave, I've got a couple of kids from the high school here looking for their order, but there are no bags for them. What happened to their orders?"

"I don't know. We packed everything that we had. Looks like another screw-up."

"What do you want me to tell them? They're pissed."

"Tell them we'll check and let them know tomorrow."

When Dave hung up, his father was standing there and said, "We need to have a talk, right now." Dave cringed.

Brad brought him down to the office and closed the door. Dave sat down on the sofa. Seeing the angry look on his father's face, he became frightened. He knew he was in serious trouble.

Pacing, his father said, "David, I know what you're doing. And I know it's against the law, so I don't have to tell you how upset I am. To make matters worse, you now have unhappy customers. What were you thinking?"

Dave, now contrite and scared, explained the chain of events, starting with the trip to Chinatown, and his idea to buy fireworks wholesale and make some money. "Dad, it was no big deal. The Chinese guys sell them all the time. I thought we could buy some and sell them to our friends, but everyone heard about how cheap they were and they all wanted in."

Brad Powell quietly admired his son's initiative, but he also wanted to take advantage of this teaching opportunity. "So, you decided it was okay to break the law so you can make a few dollars? Then you messed up the orders, and now you have unhappy customers. What happens if one of them goes to the police and complains to them?"

Stammering, he answered, "W-w-well, I, I never thought of that. You don't think they would, do you?"

"Why not? They feel like they got gypped. And I don't blame them. You also have fireworks in the house, putting me at risk."

"We buy fireworks every year in Chinatown, and we never get in trouble."

"But now you're selling them. That's illegal. And what are you going to do about your classmates who didn't get their orders, or who got shortchanged?"

Dave was surprised that his dad knew about all the problems they encountered, but he answered honestly. "I really don't know what to do."

"Well, I'll tell you what to do. You are going to give them some of your firecrackers or give them their money back. And, you'll give them all a little extra because you caused them to be dissatisfied. Yes, that hurts, but you made the mistakes, not them. So, you have to suffer the consequences, not them. Agree?"

"Yeah, Dad, you're right. We'll make it up to them."

Sitting down across from his son, he said, "Good. I expect nothing less from you. Now, I want you to think about this experience. There are important lessons here, as important as anything you will ever learn in school. I've taught you to be honest and you should never deviate from that, despite the pain it causes. Do you accept that rule?"

"Yes, but I didn't know what to do when this happened."

"What else did you learn?"

"I really like being in business, but I won't ever do anything illegal again. I was so scared every time the doorbell rang."

Brad had all he could do to keep a straight face. "And here's one more thing you may not have thought of. It's great to be in your own business, but you must set it up right and be ready to handle problems. And your customers must get more than they expect, or they may never come back. Now, go make them happy."

Relieved, Dave went up to his room. *My dad is so smart. Now I have to fix this. But it's going to hurt, a lot.*

CHAPTER 6

Keeping a Low Profile

AT THE END of Dave's seventh-grade semester, his teacher and the school principal held conferences with each student's parents in preparation for selecting high schools. He accompanied his mother and father to the meeting where they received an evaluation of his performance. Slumped in a chair at the conference table in the principal's office, Dave dreaded being there. He knew Mother Superior Lisa Carmel didn't like him, and he despised the short, overweight dictator. She gave him no slack. She always had that crabby look. He was certain that physically, she couldn't smile.

His teacher Sister Anna, who was taller, thinner, and much younger than the principal, told his parents what they already knew, that Dave was an outstanding student. But then she revealed his faults. Sister said, "I'm disappointed that he doesn't make the effort to reach his full potential. While he had the highest grades among the boys, his homework is often incomplete and hastily prepared. He is attentive in class and his spontaneous answers are always correct. But yet, he never puts in any extra time to excel."

His parents frowned and looked down at Dave as they learned about his lack of initiative.

Sister explained further. "For most students, this would be acceptable. But David has much more to offer. He could be exceptional."

With a grim stare at Dave, Mother Superior Lisa chimed in, "The one issue that the report cards do not indicate is his discipline. David clowns around in class, frequently speaking out with his unsolicited comments. He has this compulsion to entertain the other students."

Upset by this news, his mother turned to Dave and asked, "Is this true?"

Trying to quash a smirk, he answered, "Mom, I'm really not that bad. Honest. And the kids love my jokes. Even the teachers laugh."

Mother Superior continued. "Oh, there's more. His behavior has had him in my office on more than one occasion for his mischief. And there were rumors that he was selling firecrackers in the schoolyard. We know he has the skills for something like that. Had he been caught, he would have been immediately expelled."

Dave smoldered. *She had to bring all this up? This is why I hate nuns.*

The principal's comments had the desired effect on Virginia, who was shocked as she knew nothing about the fireworks venture. She looked sharply to Dave, but he feigned ignorance, shrugging his shoulders, and said nothing. She wasn't fooled as her anger flared and she exhaled loudly.

After some additional questions from Brad and Virginia, Sister Anna wrapped up the meeting with her recommendation, "For David to be successful, he needs discipline. I am urging you to consider a military academy for his high school studies."

And Mother Superior added, "Without restraint and respect for authority, he will fail in life. And that would be a shame."

Dave's disappointed parents marched him out of the building with stern looks on their faces. He could feel their anger. When they got back home, they sat him down in the upstairs living room to discuss the meeting. Virginia jumped in immediately. "What was this about selling fireworks?"

Before Dave could answer, Brad responded, "It's okay. I know about it. It was something the kids were doing, and Dave and I already discussed it in depth."

"And the discipline issue? What do you have to say about that?"

"Look, Mom. School is a bore. I look for ways to make everyone laugh and keep them from falling asleep. The nuns act like we're all stupid. I get straight A's without working at it. They could teach me everything in those six hours each day. Why should I have to do homework? It just means they didn't do their job."

Virginia was about to answer, but Brad said, "If he can get top scores without the extra study, then I agree with him. However, the discipline is absolutely essential. A military school makes sense."

"No, Dad. I don't want to go to an army school. I hate guns."

"Even more reason to attend an academy. Everyone should learn to handle guns, to respect them. But before we reach any conclusions, we'll visit some schools over the summer and make our decision together. How does that sound?"

"Well, we'll go check it out, but I can't see me marching around with a rifle."

In July, after visiting a few potential private high schools, the family went to Oakdale, Long Island to attend an open house at LaSalle Academy. The campus was immaculate and meticulously maintained. Every blade of grass appeared to be trimmed individually. But it was all wasted on Dave. With his head down and shoulders slumped, his body language showed his disinterest.

Upon arriving, all the guests were seated in the school's athletic stadium. Led by the honor guard, the drum and bugle corps came marching onto the field playing "The Battle Hymn of the Republic." This roused the entire crowd in the stands, including Dave.

Following an impressive display of music and precision marching, the group halted at center field and the band played the national anthem. Experiencing goosebumps, everyone stood for the anthem and The Pledge of Allegiance. Dave trembled at this moving welcome. *I wasn't expecting anything like this.*

The school chancellor stepped to the microphone, stood at attention, and addressed the potential candidates and their parents. Following an uplifting speech on honor, achievement, and leadership that had everyone's heart racing, the drum and bugle corps marched off the field playing "Star & Stripes Forever," ending the ceremony.

Chilled by the pageantry, Dave stood there in awe. *Wow! I want to be part of this.*

The Powells then toured the beautiful buildings and learned some of the history of the cherished institution. Driving back to Manhattan, Dave announced that he had decided that he was going to apply to LaSalle and was certain he would be accepted.

"What changed your mind, son?" Brad asked.

"Dad, I didn't expect it to be like this. The whole thing was exciting. It made me want to be there. And I have the grades to make it."

"Well, it takes more than high marks. They will look at your disciplinary record, which is shaky, at best."

"Then, I have to be better in school."

CHAPTER 7

Becoming a Plebe

T HERE WAS MUCH to celebrate in September of the following year. It started when Dave began his studies at LaSalle Military Academy. He was proud that his behavior in grammar school improved to the point that Mother Superior wrote a strong endorsement supporting his application to the prestigious school. He was certain it had been a critical component of his acceptance, overcoming the high demand for attendance at the respected academy.

After getting settled into his spartan dorm room with its utilitarian furniture, he met the three other freshmen who were to be his roommates. They were all well-dressed from affluent families and did not take much interest in him. They made him feel like he didn't belong, something Dave had never experienced before. *When I make money, you can bet I won't ever act like that.*

He spent the rest of the week in orientation. He learned about the military procedures he was required to follow, the locations of each of his classes, and all the other facilities. He strutted around the campus with his head held high. Just being there was an accomplishment he had worked hard to achieve.

The freshmen were then introduced to all the athletic programs, the many student clubs, and the other campus activities. Most impressive was the massive library housing thousands of books. Dave was attracted by the presentations of the coaches of the various sports. Although he was an accomplished swimmer and basketball player, he knew he wasn't tall enough for basketball, and his interest in swimming was waning. He became infatuated with the archery program, asking how he could join the team.

Afterward, the coach spoke to him privately about his interest in archery. Since he had no experience with this sport, he was offered an opportunity to train under one of the seniors on the team. When he showed up to watch archery practice, he met Charlie Shuford, a senior and the team's leading scorer. Charlie began to tutor Dave on the basics of archery and the practice regimen that made him the team leader. Under his direction, Dave's enthusiasm quickly enabled him to become so proficient he made the team in his second year.

Dave and Charlie became fast friends even off the archery range. Dave was not troubled by his roommates ignoring him, as Charlie proved to be a much better companion on campus. He brought him to parties and events on the weekends, and they talked frequently during the week. Dave really enjoyed hanging out with the upperclassmen.

CHAPTER 8

A Relationship for the Ages

THE SAME WEEK Dave began school, Brad got a huge promotion at IBM. After spending 15 years in Finance, he was named International Currency Manager for Central and South America, plus the Caribbean. His first task was to meet the key banking executives in his service region to determine which institutions would become business partners with IBM. Mapping out his itinerary, he decided to start with the smaller countries, and then move on to the major countries of South America. Within a week, he left for a tour of the Caribbean to interview bankers at selected financial institutions.

Brad began with the furthest island countries like Curaçao and Aruba and ended with the Bahamas. After a dozen cities visited and interviews conducted with the leading bankers, he was glad to arrive at his last stop in Nassau. For the most part, his meetings were with stodgy and, in some cases, politically appointed arrogant bureaucrats. They were all more interested in impressing him with their corner offices than discussing serious business. Brad always had difficulty interacting with self-important people whose sole accomplishment was having a title.

In Nassau, the capital of the Bahamas, Brad met with Richard Guerrero, President of Bahamas Bank, LTD. He was a tall, handsome man who spoke with a Caribbean patois. His strong features and penetrating black eyes commanded attention.

The two men hit it off immediately, as Guerrero was very different from the other executives Brad met on the fact-finding trip. This was partly due to Guerrero's attending Brad's alma mater, NYU, and being familiar with the mores of Americans, particularly New Yorkers. Even Guerrero's office was unlike that of the other CEOs. It was smaller, less opulent, and gave the impression that real business was conducted there.

Following their meeting, he invited Brad to dinner that evening. At 7 p.m., Guerrero picked him up at his hotel and brought him to a tiny restaurant on the north coast called Molly's. It was like walking into an islander's cottage home.

When they entered the small dining room, Brad noticed that he was the only white person there, including the diners, the staff, and Molly herself. She was an elderly woman who moved around gracefully and greeted Guerrero with a hug and a kiss. When introduced to Brad, he reached out for a handshake, but instead she pulled him in with a hug and welcomed him to her bistro.

The two men sat at a corner table sipping premium rum while being pampered by Molly with interesting local appetizer dishes. These included stuffed Caribbean crab, conch ceviche, and sautéed sea snails. Later in the evening, Guerrero ordered grouper, a fish Brad had never heard of. With the two men barely able to consume anything else, Molly presented her famous flan. It was so wonderful, they wolfed it down like they hadn't eaten in a week.

Guerrero ended the dinner by ordering two snifters of Pierre Ferrand Cognac. After agreeing to use Bahamas Bank as IBM's transfer facility, Guerrero suggested to Brad that he open a personal account at the bank for future use. He explained with a smile, "There may be a time in the future you want to protect some money from the prying eyes of your government."

Humoring him, Brad agreed, thinking it was more of a gesture of friendship. Guerrero also invited him to return to the island for a vacation with his family. The two men formed a close bond over dinner and Brad had no idea how important that relationship would become in years ahead.

CHAPTER 9

Christmas Break

WHEN DAVE'S CLASSES ended the week before Christmas, Brad was in Rio de Janeiro meeting with the banker who handled the IBM account. He was due home in two days. Dave took the train from school to Penn Station where his mother greeted him with a hug and a kiss. Virginia kept an arm around him as they walked through the cavernous station, with Dave carrying a suitcase full of dirty clothes and feeling awkward by her public display of affection.

In the taxi, Virginia studied his face, noticing how his looks were starting to mature. The school required a short haircut for all students. With his wavy curls gone, Dave appeared older. His body had increased muscle tone and he stood more erect. *I'm not ready for my young boy to become a man.*

With the washing machine going, Virginia made lunch for the two of them. Every time she passed his chair, she touched his shoulder or patted his cheek. Dave continued to feel uncomfortable.

"Mom, why are you touching me like that?"

"I miss you, David. It's so quiet around here without you. I'm so happy to have you home."

Over lunch, he told her about his adventures at school and how different it was living there. "Everything is so disciplined, particularly for the freshmen. It's not just the teachers ordering you, it's the upper classmen, as well."

"Knowing you, that sounds impossible. How did you manage?"

"It was hard in the beginning, but now I like it. The structure has made me think differently. I don't feel like a kid anymore."

Laughing, she said, "You'll always be *my* kid."

Dave told her about his three roommates and how they made him feel like he wasn't good enough to share a room with them. "I guess having money does that to people."

"Not always. It's more about the way they were raised."

"Well, I'm going to make a lot of money when I go into business, but I don't want to be like them."

"You never will. It's not who you are."

In the afternoon, Dave called George and learned there was a dance at the school auditorium that evening. The boys decided to go, even though neither of them wanted to be in the presence of the nuns who always hovered over the kids at the dances.

When they arrived, the auditorium was packed with his former classmates, as well as boys and girls from previous graduating classes. Dave and his friends hung out in a group, as did most others. Around the perimeter of the dimly lit gymnasium were clusters of girls and similar groups of boys, with very few people dancing. When Dave and George walked over to the refreshment table, they encountered Marianne Clark, one of their grammar school classmates.

After sharing stories of their high school experiences, Marianne asked Dave to dance. He was clumsy on the floor as he had very little experience dancing. She led him around and he enjoyed having her in his arms. He kept inhaling her fragrance, and when they danced close, he could feel her small breasts bumping his chest. But then, one of the nuns walked by, leaned into them and said, "Not so close. Leave some room for the Holy Ghost."

That killed the mood, so Dave took her to a table where they sat down and talked. They spent most of the rest of the evening getting to know each other better, with Marianne leading the conversation.

When the dance ended at 11 p.m., George came up to them and

said, "The guys are going to the deli on the avenue for a soda. You want to come?"

Dave looked over and said, "No. I'm going to walk Marianne home."

When they got to her house, Dave stood there, not knowing what to do next. Laughing nervously, they looked at each other, and Marianne pulled him in and kissed him briefly. She then turned and ran up her front stairs, saying, "Good night. See you again."

Walking home, Dave thought, *Jeez, that was awful. I feel like such a slug. I didn't know what to do. She had to lead me along like a puppy dog.*

The next morning, Dave was having breakfast in the kitchen when his mother came in, hugged him and asked, "So, how was the dance?"

"It was fun. I got to see most of my classmates from grammar school. And I danced with one of the girls, but I felt gawky."

"Why, can't you dance?"

"Not really. I mean I know some of the steps, but I'm not good. And it wasn't just the dancing. I felt funny, just walking her home. I didn't know what to do."

Suppressing a smile, she said, "We'll have to fix that. After breakfast, I'll teach you some dance steps. But let's talk about how to behave around a girl."

Blushing, Dave answered, "Mom, do we have to?"

"Of course, we do. You, my born leader, need to know what's appropriate when you're with a girl. Affection is something to appreciate and share when you have feelings for the person. And yet, you were uncomfortable when I was showing my affection for you."

"But you're my mom."

"So what? Did you feel the same way when this girl touched you?"

"Yeah. I guess you're right."

"Men enjoy when a woman shows her love. Boys, on the other hand, are embarrassed by it."

"That's the way I felt."

"David, I have always hugged and kissed you. I'm surprised you still find it awkward."

"It goes back to that kindergarten incident. I'm still troubled by that."

"Then let's talk about it. Walk me through what went through your mind."

"It was the first day of kindergarten. All the boys were seated along one wall and all the girls on the other. I noticed this girl. She was the prettiest thing I've ever seen. When Sister Louise walked out of the room, I ran over and kissed her. And when Sister walked back in and saw me, she was horrified. She brought me to the principal's office, and I sat there until you came to get me."

"I remember. Tell me how you felt about the experience?"

"Kissing the little girl felt right. But Sister's reaction made me feel like I did the most awful thing. A mortal sin. In front of every kid in the class. It still bothers me."

"Okay, under the circumstances it was innocent, but misplaced, affection. Now you're at the age where you are going from a boy to a man. So, start getting comfortable when you show your feelings. I'm going to keep doing it to you and you'll see how fast you start looking forward to it."

"I don't think I can get used to you touching me, but we'll see."

"And one more thing. What I'm describing to you is a very powerful emotion. Always make sure it's real and you never share it unless you're expressing true feelings. Never lead a girl on if you don't have those feelings for her. She will get the wrong message and expect you are more serious about her than you are. And the deeper you go, the stronger her belief that you are sincere."

"You mean, if I just hold hands or kiss a girl?"

"Yes. It starts there and grows with each step. Boys are more casual about it, and girls take it more seriously."

Later that morning, Virginia turned on the music and invited

Dave to dance. She showed him the jitterbug steps, telling him to listen to the beat of the music. He quickly caught on as he was used to being light on his feet from playing basketball. In no time, he was leading her.

She then put on some slow music and showed him the fox trot steps. Taking him in her arms, she guided him around the floor. Once he got past the closeness with his mother, he did fine and enjoyed it. She ended the dance with a big hug.

After lunch, Dave called Marianne and asked her if she'd like to meet him for a soda. They met at Woolworth's and sat at the counter sipping egg creams. He told her about his dance lessons with his mother that morning. She was delighted and said, "Hey, you want to come over to my house and practice dancing?"

"Oh, I don't know."

"Why not? Both my parents work. We'll have the whole house to ourselves."

Dave paid for the sodas, and they walked over to her place. Down in her basement, Marianne turned on her record player. She was really impressed with how much better Dave did the jitterbug. He really got into it. After a few fast dances, they took a break, and then she put on a few slow numbers. Dave easily led her around the room, pulling her in close.

When the music ended, he continued to hold her. She reached up and kissed him passionately. The reaction it caused was like nothing he felt before. His heart pounded and he had a strong sensation in his lower abdomen. He kissed her again, pulling her in tight. This time, she pressed her stomach against his groin, and he trembled. Breaking the embrace, she took his hand and led him to the couch where they sat necking for more than half an hour.

They were both aroused, and Marianne decided it was time to end the session before it went too far. They kissed once more at the front door before he left and made a date to meet the next afternoon.

That night Brad returned home, delighted to be back and looking forward to celebrating Christmas with his family. He also had news about his banking associate from the Bahamas, Richard Guerrero. Rich was coming to New York right after Christmas and had made plans to take Brad and his family to dinner during the week.

The next day Dave went to Marianne's house, and it was a repeat of the previous afternoon. They danced, and then they sat on the couch and necked. This time she took Dave's hand and laid it over her breast. His body again felt that same charge as he fondled her. They were both more aroused than the day before and Marianne rolled on top of him unbuttoning her blouse and rubbing her torso against his. She pushed her tongue into his mouth, creating a new sensation, but that triggered an unexpected reaction in his head. He gently pushed her back and sat up. She asked, "Is everything okay?"

"I can't describe the exciting feeling I have right now, but an alarm bell is going off. I think we're going too far."

"It's okay. I really want to be with you."

"But that's the problem. I'm going back to school in less than two weeks. I won't see you for months. We have to slow down."

She began to sob. "I will wait for you."

"Look, I really like you. Let's have some fun together. But we can't go all the way."

Marianne continued to cry, and Dave held her as they rocked back and forth on the couch. Finally, she calmed down and said, "You're right. It just felt so good. Let's keep seeing each other but go easier."

When Dave left and walked back home, he thought, *I can't believe I was able to stop. It was the last thing I wanted to do. I wanted to do it so bad, but I couldn't get Mom's words out of my head.*

❋ ❋ ❋

When Dave and his parents arrived at Victor's, a new Cuban restaurant further uptown, Rich Guerrero was waiting for them. The *matre'd* brought them to the table, where he rose, took Virginia's hand, and kissed her on the cheek. He shook hands and hugged Brad, and turned to Dave, saying, "So, you are the young entrepreneur. Delighted to meet you, Dave."

As Rich shook his hand, Dave was speechless. He was shocked that this stranger knew about his fireworks venture, and he couldn't believe how tall he was. Recovering, he said, "You are really tall. Did you play basketball in school?"

"Yes, I did, in high school and junior college in Nassau. Do you like basketball?"

"Yeah, I play a lot, mostly against the older kids. I'm pretty good."

"Oh, are you? Do you think you can beat me?"

"There's no way I can take a jump shot over you, but I can run circles around you with my moves and dribbling."

Laughing out loud, Rich answered, "Can you now? I doubt that. Tomorrow, we're playing one-on-one. And we'll see what you've got."

Dinner was extraordinary. Rich kept ordering special dishes and expensive wines, and the Powells were overwhelmed. Some of the appetizers were extraordinary, like Cuban beef pastries and deviled crab croquettes, but Dave couldn't stop eating the plantains. He had never experienced a restaurant dinner like that and couldn't believe the constant flow of dishes. The conversation was lively, with Rich asking Virginia about her practice, and Dave about what he learned from the fireworks deal. He also asked him, "Do you have any plans for your next venture?"

Dave beamed at the attention and answered, "Not until I finish school." Then, reconsidering, he added, "Unless some terrific opportunity comes along."

Richard and Brad both laughed at his spunk.

The next day, Rich showed up at their house ready to challenge Dave on the basketball court. They went to the park, warmed up, and began the competition. First, they played Around the World, each taking shots from ten spots around the key. They tied at nine each.

For a tiebreaker, they took three shots each from center court. Dave scored two and Rich only one. Brad and Virginia had walked up to the park to watch the competition and cheer their son on.

Next, they played One-on-One. Dave took the ball out first and sank a jumper from the top of the key, as Rich laid back, closer to the net. Rich took the ball next and scored a short jumper to tie. Dave easily dribbled around him to score but Rich's height advantage ruled the game. He scored on a jump shot to win the game.

Walking back to the house, Virginia told Dave how proud she was. "I never get to see you play basketball, but you stood up to Mr. Guerrero and gave him a run for his money."

Rich had his arm around Dave's shoulder. "You're pretty good for a little guy."

"I'm just pretty good. Period. You should have kicked my ass, but I can shoot and dribble, and I'm fast."

"We'll do this again, but next time I'll practice my long shots and bury you."

"But I'll be taller."

They both laughed and Rich hugged him. A bond formed between this man and boy that would continue for decades.

The winter break was coming to an end. Rich returned to the Bahamas, Brad went back to the office, and Virginia resumed her therapy sessions. Dave spent one more afternoon with Marianne before returning to school. It was a Christmas vacation he would never forget.

CHAPTER 10

The Adirondack Expedition

THE FOLLOWING JUNE, Dave finished his first year at LaSalle, making the honor roll with an average grade score in the mid-nineties. He was also advised by the archery coach that if he joined the team in his next semester, he would make the varsity squad. The coach told him he had a natural affinity for the sport, which he could carry to college for a scholarship after he graduated. Dave was always blessed with self-confidence, something his parents instilled in him. But his accomplishment in his first year at LaSalle against the formidable competition of some of the brightest student minds in the New York area greatly enhanced his esteem.

His parents were thrilled. Brad, with his arm around Virginia, said, "You did it, son. You turned it around. That says volumes about your mental toughness."

Virginia, in particular, praised his achievements, telling him, "David, you matured over the last two years, showing us you can reach your potential. We are so proud of you."

Dave was delighted that his efforts had paid off. Beaming, he thought, *Wow! I impressed my mom. She is so tough to please. I'm on my way.*

As a reward for his outstanding performance, Brad took him to Abercrombie & Fitch on Madison Avenue and bought him a top-line recurve bow and twelve dozen arrows. He also purchased a large tent, sleeping bags, and other camping equipment. It was Dave's first time in the iconic sporting goods store, and he was mesmerized by the vast array of high-quality goods for every sport imaginable.

Brad then planned a week-long father-and-son vacation to Adirondack Park in upstate New York. It would be an opportunity to spend time exploring the rugged, unspoiled mountains with Dave. *I'm more excited than he is about this bonding opportunity.*

Before leaving, he contacted Simon, a neighborhood handyman who did odd jobs for the residents on the street. Brad asked him to keep an eye on the house as Virginia would be home alone while they were gone.

Brad chose Indian Lake, as his parents had taken him to the sparsely populated small town in the central Adirondacks in 1938. Brad had never forgotten the pristine beauty of its vast wilderness or the warmth of the rugged mountain people. His parents had planned to build a vacation home there after the war, but they both died in a hit-and-run car accident on the Taconic Parkway in Westchester County while he was in his final year in college.

Although the mountain area with its lakes and rivers was extraordinarily beautiful, the long driving distance had discouraged frequent trips there. Brad's parents took him there only twice, but the lengthy vacations allowed him to explore the surrounding area and learn about its abundant wildlife and magnificent vistas.

The Hudson River, which originates at Lake Tear in the Clouds in Keene, New York flows through Indian Lake on its long trek past New York City to the Atlantic Ocean. The river is so remote and unblemished in the upstate region, you can walk twenty-five miles along its banks and not pass a bridge, a house, or any manmade structure.

The wilderness preserves on the south and west sides of the town are equally untouched by man. A trek across the Little Moose Mountain Wilderness or Siamese Ponds Preserves require a 30- to 40-mile excursion before signs of civilization emerge.

There are dozens of lakes and ponds in Indian Lake, with its namesake being the largest at fifteen miles long and up to 150 feet deep. Lake Abanakee, named after the local Indian tribe, drains into the Indian River and feeds into the Hudson River.

The entire region was known for its abundant wildlife, including deer, bear, beaver, coyote, and small game, plus wild turkey, hawks, partridge, and other birds. Fishing offered bass, northern pike, trout, and various panfish.

The village of Indian Lake sat at the intersection of Routes 28 and 30 and was anchored by a small Grand Union supermarket, Gibby's General Store, a pharmacy, two gas stations, and several bars.

The anticipation of his return to this untamed country after the long absence and introducing it to his son had Brad truly excited and nostalgic.

CHAPTER 11

Experiencing the Wilderness

EVEN WITH THE PREDAWN start, the drive took the entire day. As expected, Dave became restless and fidgety. Brad kept telling him of all the beautiful places of interest they would encounter. But all Dave could think about was using his powerful new bow and camping in their spacious tent from Abercrombie.

They arrived at about six in the evening. Driving into the tiny village, their first stop was the Grand Union to buy some provisions. They then drove back to the small hotel on the bank of Lake Abanakee at the bridge on Route 28. Brad booked a room for the night, and they had dinner in the small bar area where the walls of knotty pine displayed deer heads and mounted pike. Dave was fascinated by the wildlife specimens around the room and walked around examining them up close.

The hotel owner was an elderly gentleman named Clyde. He had a weather-beaten face, a bald head, and small gray eyes that were animated with smile lines. He asked about their plans and, when he heard where they were going to camp, mentioned a couple of fishing holes along the Indian River.

Early the next morning, Brad drove out Chain Lakes Road, past the Abanakee Dam. He found a clearing where they pitched camp alongside the churning rapids of the fast-moving Indian River. Once the tent was up and a firepit was built, Dave wanted to shoot his new bow. Recognizing his son's anticipation and excitement about the sleek weapon, he postponed his plan to explore the immediate area with him.

Brad had bought two large canvas tarps at Abercrombie, one for the floor of the tent, which he set up under the sleeping bags. The other he tied to two trees. This one they used as a backstop for the blunt-tipped, target arrows. They set up a target in front of it. After Dave showed his dad the proper stance and hold for releasing an arrow, they took turns shooting. Brad became frustrated as he struggled to hit the target. Dave, with his constant smile, was nearly flawless.

After the first round of shots, Dave further instructed his father on drawing the catgut bowstring back, breathing, and positioning his hand correctly. After a few more tries, Brad began to hit the target, but not nearly as often as Dave, even from his position closer to the target.

Late that afternoon, Brad taught Dave the basics of stream fishing in the Indian River. He emphasized stealth and patience, as the wary fish could easily see movement above the water. It took Dave a while to become patient and cautious as he approached the quiet coves through the brush along the river.

The next day, Brad looked for some of the fishing holes Clyde mentioned. They climbed down the rocks along the shoreline and found a few. Brad reminded Dave about what he taught him the day before. His effort paid off and they caught six large rainbow trout. With his first catch, Dave gushed with excitement from the feeling of something live that he couldn't see yanking and bending his lightweight fishing rod. "Dad! It feels like a shark is pulling on my line."

The thrill continued with each successive catch. Brad beamed as he watched his son in admiration, cheering him on and instructing him on how to land the fish.

Back at the campsite, Brad taught Dave how to gut the fish, explaining that the trout did not need to be scaled. They cooked three of the fish for dinner and packed the other three in the ice chest for a second dinner. After they ate, Dave practiced his archery. Then, exhausted, he crawled into the tent and slept soundly.

Over the next few days, they hiked the mountains, rented boats to explore lakes, and even hired a local guide named LeRoy Spring to give them fly fishing lessons. LeRoy also took them to some hidden ponds that required a hike through thick underbrush. He enjoyed training them on navigating the wilderness and Dave's growing fascination with the constant discoveries. Seeing LeRoy's reaction, Brad invited him to join them for dinner in town the following night.

Each day, Dave was awed by the encounters with nature that were so different from New York City. He loved seeing the lack of development and the vast, green-carpeted mountain range. From the tops of Snowy Mountain and Blue Mountain, they saw unspoiled virgin forests and sparkling lakes for miles all around them.

One morning they walked around a pond created by a beaver dam. After sitting quietly for a few minutes, they saw the beavers at work, strengthening the dam with logs and branches that they cut with their teeth.

While hiking through the valleys between the peaks, Brad pointed out the signs of wildlife. Deer tracks were everywhere, as were their excreted pellets. Dave was amazed when they came across bear droppings, hawk feathers, shredded fur where a fox or coyote had killed a squirrel or a snowshoe rabbit, plus other signs of life in the forest.

At one point while hiking through some brush, they were startled by a heart-stopping explosion of noise when they flushed a flock of partridge hiding in the bushes. Astonished, Dave asked, "How could a handful of birds make a sound so loud? It was like instant thunder."

On another day, Brad took Dave into a pine forest. They sat down on the pine straw in a quiet and peaceful clearing among the tall evergreens that were planted during the Great Depression. Even in this small clearing the treetops provided a canopy that filtered the sunlight. Brad asked softly, "Look around and tell me what you see and what you hear?"

Dave whispered back, "Dad, it's quieter than being in church with the nuns. There's nothing here."

"Okay, let's sit here without making a sound and see what happens."

Gradually, the forest came to life, and they could hear the chatter of birds and squirrels. As they sat still, a rabbit came right up to them, raised its ears, and hopped away. A red-tailed hawk glided through the trees and began screeching to panic the small game, and everything went quiet again. Soon the chatter returned and became even louder with red squirrels scurrying around the ground. When Brad and Dave stood up, it all went quiet again.

The end of the trip came too soon. On Saturday morning, they broke camp and began packing everything they brought in. Brad explained, "This is God's living room. You always leave it exactly the way you found it."

They scattered the rocks used for the firepit and buried the ashes. As Brad began loading the gear in the car, he handed a half-filled trash bag to Dave and said, "Police the site."

"What do you mean?"

"Pick up anything on the ground that we brought in, including any bottle caps and paper scraps."

With the site returned to its natural state, they drove up past the village to a spot along the road with vistas of the majestic peaks. They got out and looked around one last time, and Brad said, "Let's say goodbye to the mountains. But we will be back, and we'll bring mom. I promise."

"Soon, I hope. I love it here."

They then drove to the town dump and dropped off the bags of trash they had accumulated. It was mid-morning when they began the long ride home. The entire way, Dave talked incessantly about everything he experienced. Breathlessly, he said, "It is so different from living in the city. And yet, the woods are just as busy." And he longed to go back.

Basking in his son's joy, Brad couldn't wait to tell Virginia about the trip and Dave's fascination with the wilderness.

Dave, likewise, couldn't wait to tell his mother about the fun they had and everything he learned about the mountains. His excitement was overwhelming. "Mom's not going to believe all the things we did. And the wildlife! We were so close to so many different animals, right in the woods, where they live. Dad, we've just got to bring her next time."

CHAPTER 12

Euphoria Shattered

KNOWING IT WOULD BE LATE when they arrived home, Brad stopped for an early dinner at a roadside restaurant near Kingston. They quickly ate bowls of stew, anxious to get home to Virginia. Both father and son couldn't wait to share their stories.

Arriving back in the city, it was nearly 11 p.m. when they turned onto their street. Brad immediately saw the flashing lights of police cars in front of their house. He pulled up and said to Dave, "Stay in the car and don't move."

He jumped out and Simon the handyman ran up to him with tears streaming down his face. "Oh, Mr. Powell. How awful! It's your wife; she is gone."

Before he could say anything, a uniformed police officer came up to Brad and asked, "Sir, can you identify yourself?" Brad was too stunned to answer. He was in shock but had the presence to look back and make sure Dave was still in the car. Seeing the fear on his son's face, he raised his hand in a *stop* motion.

Simon answered the officer. "He's Mr. Powell, sir, the husband."

The policeman took Brad into the house through the ground floor foyer entrance where he was met by a plainclothes officer. "Mr. Powell, I'm Detective Arnie Mitchell. I'm so sorry for your loss." As he was speaking, Brad was looking around at the front office.

It was in complete disarray. Everything on the desk was scattered on the floor, and he noticed that the IBM typewriter was missing. The upholstered chair that Virginia used to interview her patients was knocked over, and there were bloodstains all over the couch and puddled on the floor. With anger overwhelming him, he shouted, "My Virginia! What happened to her? Who did this? Oh, God!"

Mitchell explained that she was found dead and taken by ambulance to the morgue for an autopsy. Brad was holding the door jamb with his head down trying to hold back the tears. Mitchell took him by the arm, led him upstairs to the living room, and sat him down.

"Can I get you something, water, coffee?"

"My son. Dave is in the car outside. Someone, please get him."

By now, Dave was panic-stricken and crying uncontrollably, trying to imagine what had happened. He cried out, "Where's my mom? Where is she?"

Another uniformed officer came out to the car and brought Dave in through the front door at the top of the stoop. Brad jumped up and hugged his son. "Oh, David. Something terrible has happened to Mom. She's gone."

Before he could say more, Dave slumped in his arms, sobbing and shaking. They sat down on the living room sofa across from the detective, with Brad hugging his son. They cried together with Dave holding his father tightly.

Mitchell explained to them that there had been a break-in through the downstairs door. "Apparently, Mrs. Powell had been at her desk last evening when the intrusion occurred. Your caretaker noticed the downstairs door open late this morning, and when he went to check, he discovered her body in the office. He called us right away.

"The investigation is ongoing, and we're locking off the entire downstairs until the officers complete their work down there. An autopsy is being performed and will be completed tomorrow, but we would like you to identify the body. Can we send a car to pick you up at ten a.m. tomorrow?"

They were both in shock and had difficulty absorbing all these details. Brad continued to hold Dave but realized that he had to pull himself together for his son's sake and for his needed participation in this investigation.

Finally, after the police left, Brad took Dave up to the master bedroom so they could sleep together. He gave him one of Virginia's sleeping pills to help him get through the night.

Once Dave was asleep, Brad went down to the living room and anxiously paced the floor. He sobbed quietly for about an hour. *How can I carry on without Virginia? How is Dave going to survive without his mother?* He thought about the plans he made with Dave to bring Virginia to the mountains. And he cried more.

Brad and Virginia had a special relationship. In the beginning, he had been somewhat detached and had difficulty communicating with her. As a psychologist, she taught him how to be open and share his most personal thoughts, how to discuss differences, and how to express his love for her. That brought out a deep intimacy between them. He now had a hole in his heart that could never be filled.

Toward dawn, he realized that he had to be strong. He had to protect his son and raise him without his mother. He needed to fill her role, to become both parents and hold everything together.

Brad also realized that he had to teach Dave about the vital necessity of communicating with a loved one. He sat down at the kitchen table to make a list and began thinking of everything he had to do. *This is overwhelming. It's more than a full-time job on top of my full-time job. How can I be both parents?*

CHAPTER 13

Struggling to Cope

AFTER A FITFUL NIGHT for both of them, with Brad getting only a couple of hours of sporadic sleep, he was picked up at ten o'clock and brought to the morgue. Mrs. Grabenstetter, who had watched the police activity from her window the entire previous day, had called and offered to watch Dave and help in any way she could.

The coroner brought Brad to the autopsy lab, where a wave of nausea passed over him. He was not prepared for the tortuous assault from the foul, pungent odors or the sadistic appearance of the large, windowless room. Shaking, he stood over a porcelain table holding a body covered in a sheet. The doctor slid the cover down just enough to reveal the victim's face.

Brad looked and quickly turned away as he was about to pass out. Despite the bruising, swelling, and discoloration, it was Virginia. Her face had been cleaned up, but her lower lip was split open and swollen. There were contusions on her cheeks and around her left eye. Her nose appeared broken. The coroner helped Brad out of the room and sat him down on a bench in the hall where he quietly sobbed.

Before leaving the building, Mitchell advised him that he wanted Brad to come to his office the next day where the detective would share the details of the investigation and the autopsy. Now that the crime scene was being released, he also asked Brad to search the house and prepare an inventory of what was stolen.

Brad arrived home, still dazed from everything that had transpired in the last 24 hours. Although Mrs. Grabenstetter had made breakfast for Dave, most of it was uneaten on the kitchen table where she sat quietly saying the rosary. Brad poured himself a cup of coffee and went up to his son's room.

Dave was sitting on his bed, still listless and confused. "Dad, who did this? Why did they hurt mom?"

Brad joined him on the bed and explained, "Someone broke in Friday night to rob us, and she must have tried to stop them. She was no match for whoever it was, but she must have fought hard. And she was beaten to death. I don't know why they picked our house. We have nothing special that anyone would want to steal."

"I was so excited to tell mom about our trip. And now, she's gone. She'll never know how great it was, how beautiful the mountains are." He began crying again.

Brad knew he had to keep his son occupied and not let him dwell on this devastating event. He told him about the detective's request to determine what had been stolen. "I want you to help me. Search your room to see if anything is missing. And then go through the house and make a list of items that are either missing or broken."

When he went back down to the kitchen, Mrs. Grabenstetter asked Brad if Dave was feeling any better. Responding in the negative, he then thanked her for her help.

As she was leaving, she asked, "Would you like me to come back later and prepare dinner for you?"

Touched, he hugged her and said, "Thank you so much for helping out this morning. We will need your help from time to time, but we must now learn to be on our own. I have to go to police headquarters again tomorrow morning if you can come over then. I'll also call you whenever I can't be around to take care of Dave."

With the initial shock absorbed, Dave sat in his room and began to think about how his life was going to change without his mom. Like most young boys, he'd always thought of his mother as the person who limited the joy of his activities. She'd always limited his plans and added rules that he thought unnecessary. But more recently, he'd begun to see her in a whole new light. *She was helping me be more grown up and teaching me how to act with girls. And now she's gone.*

He thought about all the times she was there when he participated in a swim meet, and when he played basketball with Mr. Guerrero. *She cheered me on and always showed me love. It used to embarrass me when she hugged me in front of my friends. But now, she's never going to hug me again.* And he began crying.

※　※　※

Checking his to-do list, Brad called his boss at home and explained the heartbreaking discovery he found when he returned from his vacation with his son. He requested a few weeks' leave to spend more time with Dave and take care of all the changes that he must now face. His boss fully understood and said, "Take all the time you need. I will call you only in an emergency."

The next call Brad made was to the funeral parlor. The director told him they would schedule the transfer of her body from the morgue, and he could come by the next day to make arrangements. He then phoned his insurance company to report the break-in and was told an adjuster would contact him.

Brad waited until the early afternoon to call the parish pastor. Father Thomas was already aware of Brad's plight and explained, "During every sermon this morning, we asked the parishioners to pray for your family. Would you like to schedule a funeral mass for later this week?"

"Yes, I would like to do it as soon as possible. Since we have no family, the attendees will just be some neighbors and a few of my co-workers."

"How is David holding up? He has a deep faith, which was bolstered by his time as an altar boy."

"He is strong, but he is struggling."

The last call he made that day was to his friend, Rich Guerrero. Brad had to let him know that he was canceling their planned vacation to Nassau. "Rich, there's been a tragedy in my home. My wife was murdered."

Shocked, Guerrero answered, "Oh, Brad, how devastating. I can't even imagine what you're going through. And I was so looking forward to hosting you when you came down for vacation. What happened?"

Guerrero listened intently as Brad became choked up taking him through the details of that horrible night. He then said, "I am here for you, no matter what you need. And that includes anything clandestine or questionable that you may be forced into. I have the connections to help you."

Brad couldn't fathom what Guerrero was suggesting. *He must mean that there was no limit to what he would do to help me.*

CHAPTER 14

The Devil Is in the Details

BRAD ARRIVED at the precinct and was greeted by Detective Mitchell. The entire office was a collection of well-worn steel and vinyl furniture. The floors were littered with debris and the desks were covered with paperwork and paper cups half-filled with stale coffee. Emphasizing the disorder, a cacophony of ringing phones reverberated through the bullpen area. Mitchell brought Brad into a small, featureless conference room where his partner and the coroner were both seated at the table.

"Mr. Powell, this was a violent home invasion that we expect began as a robbery. Our investigation shows that the vic . . . er . . . your wife was home alone working in the ground floor office. One of the neighbors told us the only light on in the house was in that room. And that was about 11:30 Friday night.

Referring to his notes, Mitchell's partner added, "Probably sometime after midnight, we're pretty certain two perpetrators broke in through the front basement door and overpowered her. They spent a substantial amount of time both searching the house for contraband and molesting your wife. There was evidence of their activity throughout the house. Dr. Lindsay will explain his findings to give you more detail on what these savages did to her."

Mitchell jumped in saying, "Yesterday at the morgue, we didn't show you the entire body, as we merely wanted you to identify her. But she was ravaged. We're sure there were two attackers, probably both male. Dr. Lindsay will share some details from his autopsy."

Lindsay looked up from his notes and began to address Brad. He had a thin face with a goatee and mustache, and he wore a lab coat. He said, "In layman's terms, the deceased had bruises on both wrists and ankles, showing where she was held. She was punched in the face multiple times, and she had cigarette burns on her abdomen and her inner thighs. Her vagina was torn from rough intercourse. The blows and burns were done to subdue her and keep her from screaming. She ultimately died from multiple stab wounds to the torso, indicating anger and rage. No weapon was found."

Brad sat there trembling with his hands over his eyes to hide his tears. He was now pale and shaken. Mitchell offered him a glass of water.

Lindsay continued, "The most heinous part of the rape was something uncovered during the autopsy examination. Her mouth was badly bruised, which we attributed to blows to the face. However, we found a piece of flesh tissue inside her mouth. It seems that she bit off a fairly large piece of the penis from one of the perps."

A wave of nausea and light-headedness overtook Brad as he fell back in his chair and nearly passed out. They moved him to a couch in the chief's office to help him recover. When he felt better, they returned to the conference room, and Mitchell provided the final details of the investigation.

"This crime was not committed by career criminals, but by amateur perps. It was probably two young males, at least one of them a negro, based on the tissue sample recovered. Be advised, it will be very difficult to make an arrest unless we capture them in another robbery.

"We will provide a police report to facilitate your insurance company's claim payment. I'll ask you to provide a complete list of missing items, and any photos you have of those items. We can then canvas pawn shops and places we know that deal in stolen merchandise."

When he was finished, Mitchell had Brad sit in the conference room a little longer to give him time to recover from the anguish and pain of the report.

Later that afternoon, Simon came over and shared a couple of beers with Brad. He was short, stocky, and bald with a full beard. Simon was a bachelor and made a living handling chores and repairs for the neighborhood residents. He also had some contractual income from merchants by being on call to do maintenance and upkeep.

Simon was angry and saddened about the home invasion and that it occurred while he was watching the house. Hugging his friend, he said, "Brad, I'm so sorry that I wasn't there when this happened. If I had passed by at that time, I could have stopped it."

"Nonsense! I didn't expect you to watch the house around the clock. It happened after midnight. No one was around to see it."

"What did the police tell you about their investigation?"

"Not much. They said it was kids, based on what was stolen, like the liquor bottles. They beat her up pretty badly, raped her, burned her with cigarette butts, and stabbed her multiple times. And there's almost no chance they will be caught. The coroner said they were negro."

"So, it was two young pricks? That's interesting. I noticed a couple of negro kids hanging around the block recently. I would recognize them if I saw them again. But you can bet they won't hit this block again. They probably moved onto another neighborhood."

"They will get caught eventually, for some other crime, but that doesn't make me feel any better. I want them punished for what they did to Virginia."

"I agree. By the way, did they take anything that could be positively identified, like a piece of custom jewelry?"

"No. We have Virginia's good jewelry in our safe. Oh, wait. They stole my typewriter. It's a prototype of a new IBM model that isn't on the market, yet."

"Can you get me a picture of it? My brother-in-law owns a pawn shop, and he's in touch with places that fence stolen goods. He can circulate it around, and maybe you'll get a hit."

CHAPTER 15

Sheltering Dave

IT WAS A TRYING SUMMER for both father and son. Over the next few weeks, Dave wandered around listlessly, yearning for his mother's presence. And Brad found it difficult to come home and not be greeted by his beautiful wife. The energy that gave the home its life was no longer there. They were both lost in the empty, joyless house.

Brad asked Mrs. Grabenstetter to look after Dave during the day, offering to pay her for her time. She refused the money but was delighted to help. Dave referred to her as Mrs. Grabby and, needing a motherly presence, began to enjoy her company. She delighted him with stories of her upbringing as a young girl in Germany and her later emigration to England and on to the United States. She also told him about her career in the Air Force.

In late July, Brad called the chancellor at LaSalle and told him about the tragic death of Dave's mother. He responded, "Yes, I read about it in the paper, and the faculty has been praying for both of you. Is there anything we can do to help your son during this difficult time?"

"Thank you, Father. And that's why I called. I have an unusual request and I'm hoping you can find a way to fulfill it. Is there any way my son can return to school early? I will gladly pay extra tuition to have him on campus. Maybe you could use him to work onsite or help with the freshman orientation weekends."

"Yes, that would help him. I'm sure we can do something along those lines. Let me speak to some of my staff and I will call you back."

The next day, Brad told Dave to pack his clothes. He was going back to school a month early to start a new job with the school's maintenance department. He would earn some spending money and be able to practice archery before the team got back.

"We leave tomorrow morning, and I will visit you every parent's weekend." Dave was thrilled about the plan and the change of environment. This reprieve would be a perfect way to begin the slow process of recovery. He thought about the opportunity. *I can use the archery range whenever I'm not working.*

With his son at school, Brad could now focus on the future and make adjusted plans for their lives without Virginia. He had been calling Detective Mitchell for updates on the investigation, and there had been no new developments. With each call, he became more incensed. *Those two bastards are getting away with torturing and murdering my wife.*

When Simon stopped by, Brad gave him a photo of the typewriter that had been stolen. "The new-products manager at the office who gave me the photo said there probably isn't another typewriter like it in the entire city. Can you give it to your brother-in-law and have him circulate it?"

"Absolutely. He'll be glad to help out."

"I will pay a reward if we can find these pricks. How about $250? Do you think that's enough?"

"That should get some action, without a doubt. Then you can take the information to the police."

Brad decided to sell his brownstone home, which had been in the family for over 40 years. He felt that they could no longer live there if he and Dave were going to get past the horror that destroyed their family life. When the realtor told him it would sell quickly, he began looking at apartments to rent.

Near the end of September, the realtor brought him a qualified offer, but the buyer wanted to negotiate the price. At first, Brad was willing to lower the asking price, but then he told the realtor to counteroffer at full price and include all the furniture and appliances. With terms agreed and a contract signed, a closing date was scheduled for the middle of December. Brad then put a deposit on a spacious concierge-attended apartment a few blocks further uptown.

Simon called him a couple of days later, excited to tell him, "Brad, they found the typewriter!"

CHAPTER 16

Private Investigation

BRAD AND SIMON drove up to a storefront on Second Avenue in East Harlem. The rusted sign hanging precariously over the door said, *General Merchandise–New & Used.* The windows were so grimy you couldn't see inside, and for good reason.

Upon entering, the two men's senses were assaulted by a filthy showroom that exuded the smell of mold mixed with stale coffee and dying rodents. The linoleum tile floor in the traffic areas was worn down to the wood planking under it, and all the merchandise was covered with a layer of dust, some of which must have dated back to the turn of the century. If Brad didn't know better, he was certain he had just entered a medieval storage dungeon.

They walked up to a cage that served both customers and vendors. Sitting behind the glass and metal barrier was an aging bald man who could barely fit in the torn leather office chair that appeared older than the dust in the showroom.

Simon introduced himself as the brother-in-law of Abe Stein who owned a pawnshop on West 32nd Street. Looking up, the proprietor in his New York Yiddish accent said, "You musta be the guy looking for the typewriter, eh? Itza right here. Vacha tink?"

Brad stepped forward, 'Yes, that's my typewriter. It's a test model and it's the only one in New York."

"I nevva seen nuthin' like it. I gava those two scumbags ten dollahs for it. Musta be worth fifty, right?"

"That's it. I'll give you $50 for it, right now."

"Oy. Nevva mine the fifty. What about the reward. It's two-hundred-and-fifty sheckles, ay?"

"Okay. How do I find the men who brought it in?

"Men? Dey were smutches, two punk kids, 16, maybe 17. All skin ana bones."

"All right, where can I find them?"

"I havva pitcher. I show you."

Seeing the photo, Simon said, "That's the two pricks I saw on the street. Where did you get a picture of them?"

Leaning in close, Abe pointed to a box set against the glass and despite the store being empty, he whispered, "Oy. Datza camra inside. I take pitchers of ever body comes ana selza me sumting."

Brad handed Abe $250 in cash and took the typewriter and the photo of the kids. The two men were excited about their unexpected haul.

Driving back downtown, Brad said, "Simon, I can't thank you enough for this."

"I'm glad I could help. Now the cops have to get off their ass, collar those two animals and put them away."

"That may not be so easy. It looks like they're underage, and the cops still have to capture them. I'm going to make a copy of this photo before I turn it in at the station."

He took the snapshot to a camera shop for an enlarged print. It was ready the next day and he brought it to Detective Mitchell's office and handed it over, saying, "These are the two scumbags that murdered my Virginia."

"What? How did you get that?"

Without mentioning Simon or the reward, Brad explained how he tracked down the unique typewriter to a shop in East Harlem and got the photo from the proprietor. He then asked, "Do you think you can catch them now?"

"Maybe we'll get lucky. Give me the address of the shop that had the typewriter. I'll send a car up there. But, Mr. Powell, don't get your hopes up. There are at least fifteen gangs running around the city. Most of them are from Harlem and they are all fighting with each other. And every teenager and young adult belongs to one of those gangs. Finding these two pricks won't be easy, but the photo will help."

Brad left the police station disillusioned by the detective's glib attitude. Mitchell seemed to be making excuses in advance for his expected failure to apprehend the two suspects. Brad vowed, *I'm going to keep the pressure on him until he arrests them and justice is done. I swear they won't get away with what they did.*

CHAPTER 17

The Plan Emerges

BRAD WAITED TWO WEEKS before calling Mitchell for an update. The detective reported that a squad car was sent to the store and a report was submitted. But since then, there had been no sightings of anyone matching the images in the photo. He promised to immediately notify Brad of any developments in the case.

Although he continued to call Mitchell regularly, Brad kept getting messages from the operator that there were no updates. Brad knew in his heart there would be no justice from the police. *These two pricks are murderers. They must be punished.*

Refusing to let them get away with this terrible crime, he now knew he had to take matters into his own hands. He sat and wrote a complex plan, covering every possible scenario to achieve his goal. His first step was to stake out the store.

He took his car up to Putnam County and drove along dirt roads until the vehicle was covered in brown dust. He stopped at a puddle along one of the roads and took handfuls of mud and splattered them on the bumpers and license plates, obscuring the letters and numbers.

For the next week, each night Brad parked his car across the street from Abe's store. On the third night, just before closing time, two black youths entered the store carrying a large box. With adrenaline flowing, he picked up a pair of binoculars off the seat and waited for them to emerge from the entrance.

When they came out, he confirmed that they were the two punks in the photo. He watched them walk along Second Avenue and turn down East 109th Street. He went back the next week, and on the first night of surveillance, he saw them again. Like the previous week, they left and walked the same route.

Knowing that the plan could now work, he met with Simon and shared it with him. He then said, "Simon, I need a partner on this, but it's dangerous and illegal. If we get caught, you'll go to jail."

Learning the details of Brad's plan, Simon became excited about being a part of this vigilante justice. He was shocked when Brad offered him $5,000 to assist him in this caper, as he was not expecting compensation. "I would do it for nothing, just to avenge Virginia's murder."

Simon had been dreaming about moving out of the city that was now becoming crime ridden. His goal was to relocate to Miami and start a handyman business there among his Jewish friends. Brad's reward money was his ticket.

After the meeting, Brad canceled his deposit on the apartment he was planning to rent. Following the closing on the brownstone, they would no longer be living in New York City.

The next call Brad made was to his friend in the Bahamas. Explaining the intricate details of his plan, he said, "Rich, I'm following up on your offer to help me with my situation in New York. I'm flying down this week. What do you need me to bring, and how long will it take to complete your work?"

"Brad, thank you for allowing me to help you. I consider it an honor. And it is a chance to repay you for all the IBM business that keeps growing for our bank. Just bring a head photo of your son. I will get everything in motion right away."

CHAPTER 18

Covering the Details

WHEN BRAD ARRIVED in Nassau, Guerrero was at the airport to meet him. His limousine drove them back to his office. Getting right down to business, he took a portrait photo of Brad and asked for Dave's photo.

"My work will take two days. I will deliver everything you need for complete identity changes for both you and Dave. The documents will include birth certificates from hospitals in Chicago. Driver's licenses for both of you, as I changed Dave's age to 18. You will also get new Social Security cards and passports. And finally, a New York concealed carry permit, should you choose to own a pistol."

"I can't believe you can create all those documents."

"Yes, and they will be authentic, so you don't have to worry. I have set up a bank account for you here. And once you close on your house, wire the funds into it, and you'll have easy access without a paper trail."

"Excellent, and I will have other funds to deposit. I'll wire them, as well?"

"Yes. And one other thing I thought of that you didn't request. I am issuing you and Dave American Express cards. You will pay for the charges through this new account I set up, and you can also draw cash from the cards as you need it."

"Why did you choose Chicago?"

"I expect you will live in a city with a low crime rate. That eliminates most of the larger cities in the US. Once you decide, you can transfer the driver's licenses to whatever home state you choose and renew them as needed. Dave will not have to take a driving test, but you'll have to teach him to drive."

"You thought of everything. This is amazing."

"I think I did, but if there's anything else you need, let me know. Now, let's go have lunch."

Two days later, Guerrero handed Brad a package of documents. "Mr. Ben Powers, it's a pleasure to meet you. And I look forward to meeting the young Mr. Dave Powers. As you can see, I kept Dave's first name. It will be easier for him to answer to the same first name and the nearly same last name."

"Rich, you covered so many more details than I thought of. I can't thank you enough."

"It is my pleasure, my friend. Now, as you liquidate all your assets, just wire transfer the money to your account here. And I will look forward to frequent visits from the Powers men. Good luck with this new venture!"

CHAPTER 19

Tasting Justice

WHEN BRAD returned to New York, he booked a suite at the Algonquin Hotel in the Times Square area for ten days. He closed on the brownstone house the following day at his attorney's office and instructed the funds to be wire transferred to his Bahamas account. The following weekend Brad would pick Dave up from school for the Christmas break, but he had a task to complete before then.

Over the last month, Brad had been meeting with his boss at IBM and with the Human Resources VP. He had announced that due to the distress of his wife's murder, he could not continue working for the company.

Because of his superior performance, plus the cause that triggered his need to retire, the company offered him a generous severance package. He took the package as a lump sum and wired the funds to his account.

He then had his stockbroker sell all his stock holdings, including his IBM shares, and transferred the funds to Nassau. The total balance would allow him and Dave to live comfortably but judiciously without other income for many years to come.

Using the gun permit, Brad (now Ben) went to a gun shop and purchased a .357 magnum pistol and a box of wadcutter ammo.

That night, he and Simon went back to East Harlem to surveil Abe's store, without success. The next night, they saw the two perps enter the store. With Simon at the wheel, they drove around the corner and parked. Brad got out and stood in the shadows.

Ten minutes later, their two targets came around the block. As they walked by the parked car, Brad stepped forward with his gun drawn. "Get in the car and don't open your mouth or I'll blow your fucking heads off."

Seeing a tall stranger with a large gun, the two youths quickly complied. Sitting in the back seat, one of them asked, "What you want wit us, man?"

Pointing the gun at them, Ben said, "I told you to keep your mouths shut."

Following the plan, Simon drove to 58th Street under the West Side Highway. They came to an open-air construction storage area that was lined with a broken cyclone fence.

Brad got out with the two thugs and told Simon to drive the car back. He then walked them to the back of the fenced-in lot cluttered with building material and construction debris.

He shined a flashlight on them and told them to drop their pants and shorts. The two confused teens were terrified by this point, and one said, "What's goin' on, man? We didn't do nuthin."

"Just shut your fucking mouth, and do what I said, now!"

Both boys dropped their pants. Brad moved the light down to their genitals and saw the scar on one of their penises. "How'd you get that scar?"

"Oh, that from a accident. It's nuthin."

"Bullshit! My wife bit it when you were raping her."

Now realizing who Brad was and what might happen next, the two boys started trembling and crying. Standing at close range, Brad pointed the gun down and shot them both in the groin. The wadcutter bullets decimated their genitals. They fell to the ground, dazed and writhing in pain. He then stood over them as they began screaming and he shot them both twice in the face. They died instantly, their faces shattered and unrecognizable from the damage of the bullets.

Ben wiped the blood splatter from himself and purposely walked away at a nonchalant pace, thinking, *Only in New York could you fire six shots from a gun along with loud screaming, and it would be ignored by everyone.*

As he walked crosstown along 57th Street, he dropped the bloodstained handkerchief in a trashcan on the sidewalk and strode to his car. When he got back to the hotel, he showered and changed his clothes, discarding the stained clothes and shoes in a shopping bag. He then wiped off the gun and wrapped it in black tape. Leaving the hotel well after midnight, he walked south a few blocks and along a deserted street. He dropped the wrapped gun in a storm drain and a couple of blocks later tossed the shopping bag in a dumpster.

Brad had avenged Virginia's torture, abuse, and murder. He accomplished what the police were too busy or too lazy to achieve. But he felt no satisfaction. *Revenge is not sweet. But at least I know those two bastards are not walking the streets and preying on any more victims.*

Exiting Gotham

THE NEXT MORNING, Brad took his car to the carwash and then traded it in for a brand-new Jeep CJ-3. From there he drove to LaSalle to pick up Dave, who was delighted with his father's choice of the new car. When they got back to the hotel, Brad ordered dinner from room service. Over dinner and beer, he related everything he had done while Dave was at school. He described how he and Simon found the two culprits, getting no cooperation from the police.

He had also learned that because the criminals were underage, they would not have spent their lives in prison, but rather just a few years in juvenile detention. That would have resulted in them becoming hardened criminals who would then resume their lives of crime. Brad described how he mapped and implemented the entire plan, plus the preparation for going forward. By the time he finished the story, including the death of the boys without the gruesome details, both Brad and his son were in tears.

"Dad, what do we do now?"

"As of now, our new life begins. And it will be a completely new life. I retired from IBM. I'm taking you out of school. I've changed our names. We're moving to Indian Lake. And we're never looking back."

"Holy crap, Dad! Do we have to do all this? What about my friends?"

"What happened to mom will affect you your whole life. To make it easier for you, and for me, we're moving out of this crime-ridden city. Living in the mountains will help us heal."

"I like the idea of going back to the mountains, but changing our lives like that is so extreme. Do we have to?"

"Without your mom, I have to be around for you these next few years. And I can't take a chance on being arrested for what I did to those boys. And you won't be able to see your friends anymore, not even George. Did you make any close friends at school?"

"I hung around with the archery team, but I wasn't that close to any of them, not like I was with George. I was closest to Charlie Shuford from the archery team, but he graduated last June, and I lost contact with him. But I really won't be able to keep in touch with George?"

"We are going to disappear into the wilderness of the Adirondacks. No one will know where we went. After a while, you will make some new friends in Indian Lake. And in a few years from now, as you become an adult, you can choose your own path."

Seeing that Dave was still troubled, he added, "Think of it as a new adventure. And that's exactly what it will be."

During the next couple of days, they shopped for heavy winter clothing and other provisions they would need during the winter in the mountains. Brad also wrote a letter to LaSalle advising them that they were moving away, and Dave would not be returning to school.

Dave took time out to visit Mrs. Grabenstetter and say goodbye. He told her they were moving away, and he wouldn't be able to see her for a long time. His father had coached him to say that they were going cross country and didn't know where they would end up. With tears in her eyes, she hugged him and told him to send his address when they found their new home. He said he would, but knew it was a promise he couldn't keep.

On Christmas day they packed the Jeep with everything they owned and had their final dinner in New York. They chose Mama Leone's, but it was very crowded, and the food and service was mediocre. Early the next morning, they left on their new journey.

PART II

Wilderness Indoctrination

CHAPTER 20

A New Beginning

On THE RIDE UP from New York City, Dave Powers was still apprehensive about what lay ahead for them. He was excited by the prospect of living in the wilderness. But how was he going to adjust to this radical change? He had always been popular, as all the kids gravitated to him. How would he survive in a small town where no one knew him? He didn't want to dampen his father's enthusiasm, but he thought, *This is scary. It will take years to make friends like I had in New York.*

Ben Powers noticed his son's discomfort during the long car ride north and began talking to him, explaining what he thought their future might look like. He talked up the hunting, fishing, camping and other activities they would be experiencing. "We're going to buy some land and build a cabin. Maybe we'll even get a boat to explore the beautiful lakes."

"What are we going to do for money if you're not working? How are we going to buy all these things?"

"Living a simple life in the Adirondacks is far more affordable than an expensive city like New York. We won't be spending money on new cars and fancy restaurants."

He then went on to explain how he transferred all their savings, the proceeds from the sale of the house, and his stock and money from IBM to Rich Guerrero's bank in the Bahamas. Guerrero was going to manage the account using investment vehicles, so it would grow. They could draw money as they needed it. He also arranged for each of them to have a credit card, which would also be paid through the bank account.

After stopping at a supermarket in Albany, Ben and Dave arrived at Indian Lake after dark. Ben had rented a small cabin along Route 30 at the edge of the village. When they got settled in, he gave Dave his driver's license and told him they would start lessons the next day. He also gave him his credit card and showed him the paperwork for the bank account in Nassau. Included was Mr. Guerrero's business card.

He added, "If anything ever happens to me, you contact Rich and he will help you with anything you need, regardless of the issue. But remember, you can never tell anyone about this bank account."

The next day, they visited the town clerk's office. It appeared to be a single-story house that had been converted to a handful of offices. Introducing themselves, Ben asked if there was any available property to purchase. The clerk welcomed them to town and mentioned that there were several parcels of land, some with cabins or outbuildings, that were available through a tax sale.

"That sounds great. We're looking for something secluded where we can observe nature and the wildlife here."

Laughing, the clerk said, "If that's what you're looking for, it will be easy around here. You can even find deer waiting at the stop sign in the middle of town. I suggest you look at this parcel down in the Beaver Meadow area. And here's a beautiful piece of property along the Cedar River that has a cabin on it that's set back in the woods."

After giving him a list of other available properties to check out, she suggested that he meet Gil Turner, the only attorney in town, who could help him with the purchase process if he found something he liked. In addition to the tax lien parcels, she pointed out that just about every privately-owned property in town had a For Sale sign on it.

Seeing Ben's questionable look, she explained. "There's not much industry here in the mountains, other than a little mining and lumbering. We're poor people who rely on vacationers, hunters, and fishermen to survive. And a handful of us have jobs with the county or the state. What you will find here is an excellent work ethic. We don't have much money, but we don't look for handouts or welfare."

Dave asked, "Are there many people my age in town?"

"Oh, there are over 100 kids in the high school. Among our young people, the smart ones go to college and never come back. Just about everyone else is doing manual labor of some kind. And, of course, we do have a few drunks. We're a sleepy little town, blessed with untold beauty, but we're gradually shrinking."

When they left the clerk's office, they both thought about what they had learned. Dave became more concerned. He said, "Dad, I'm afraid the people in town that are my age are the ones that aren't very smart. And they'll be the only ones left after high school. How am I going to make friends?"

"Why not take it a day at a time? We have no idea what the future will bring. Given all the unknowns, we'll be flexible. And we may not stay here forever. Let's enjoy the adventure and see where it takes us. At this point, we have no attachments."

Ben recognized the environment as perfect for what he was seeking, but he realized it would not satisfy Dave. They would have to discuss this in-depth and possibly adjust their long-term plan.

CHAPTER 22

Life Interrupted

AFTER SPENDING a few days visiting the suggested sites to purchase, Ben and Dave both agreed that the Cedar River property was perfect for them. It was nearly a mile off the paved road and less than two miles from the center of town. Access was at the end of an overgrown dirt track, but the dilapidated cabin was right on a bend in the river.

Not more than a shack, it was log-sided and had a kitchen open to the living area, a small bathroom that needed updating, and two bedrooms. Several of the windows were broken, and it needed paint, new shelves, and cabinets. There was trash everywhere, making the place look even more undesirable. It had the appearance of a shelter that barn animals would reject.

Ben looked at Dave, smiled, and said, "What do you think?"

"I love the setting, but the cabin?"

"I feel the same way. It will take the better part of a year to get it the way we want, but we've got nothing but time. Let's buy a new generator right away and hire a plumber to get the heat running and replace the bathroom fixtures. Then we can move in and work during the day."

After making the purchase, they went to Gibby's General Store and ordered a generator. Gibby, the owner, welcomed them to town and recommended an electrician and a plumber to do the installation and the repairs.

A few weeks later, they moved in and started replacing broken windows, adding insulation, and making the place comfortable. Ben and Dave enjoyed working together as they learned home renovations through trial and error. The process was going very slowly.

One morning LeRoy Spring, a local guide came to the cabin and greeted them. "I heard in town that you fellas bought this camp and were fixin' it up. I drove out to see if ya need any help. This time a year it's kinda slow for me."

Ben introduced himself and Dave, and invited him in. Over coffee, LeRoy made some suggestions about the repair work. Picking up on his comments, Ben said, "We could use all the help we can get. Would you be interested in working for us on this renovation project?"

"Well, I sure could use the money, but I gotta tell ya, I'm no contractor. I can make the project move faster, though."

During the harsh winter, LeRoy worked for them on weekdays, while Ben and Dave also worked on the weekends. They relaxed in the evenings and had long conversations. Ben used the time to teach Dave everything he could about business. He even ordered some business books for Dave to use for reference.

Dave absorbed the knowledge like a sponge. He was fascinated to learn about topics such as manufacturing, finance, distribution, sales, and marketing. It was like going to night school.

By April, they needed a break from the confines of the cabin and the non-stop construction. After five months of freezing temperatures, the forecast for that Sunday was warm and sunny. Ben suggested a hike to the top of Chimney Mountain as Dave had never been there before.

That morning, they parked in the small lot at the trailhead and Ben left the keys under the mat of the front seat. He explained to Dave, "It's safe to leave your keys in the car here. People don't even lock their front doors in the mountains. With the keys in the car, you won't ever lose them in the woods."

The ground was still frozen, but walkable. The trail started out wide, and as they climbed, it became narrower. Along the way, they encountered forks in the trail that led to other parts of the mountain. They explored a few, and one gave them a beautiful view of Indian Lake including the dam far below at the north end. They sat on a rock overlooking the dazzling vista and ate their lunch.

As they continued up the last leg to the summit, it clouded over and began to drizzle. The moisture made the frozen ground slippery, so they slowed down and walked more gingerly. A little further up the slope near the summit, it rained harder. To keep from getting soaked, they crawled under a giant fir tree which kept them surprisingly dry.

Seeing breaks in the clouds, Ben said, "It looks like the rain will pass soon. We'll wait it out here. We're close to the peak, and you have to see the chimney."

"The chimney? Did someone build a chimney at the top?"

"No, the glaciers did. There's a rock formation at the top shaped like a chimney, giving the mountain its name. But the most interesting features are the crater-like openings at the summit. It's similar to the top of a volcano with a series of fissures. They form a network of caves that are up to 200 feet deep. And there is snow in them, year-round."

"Wow. We have to get to the summit and see them."

When the rain stopped, they continued their trek by cautiously walking on the icy ground which had become even more glazed. Holding tree branches, they slowly advanced up to the rock face, reaching the summit. Dave was awed by the huge rock formations. The stunning chimney rose above the summit area like a sentinel. The sun was now out, and the wind picked up, but the ground was still slippery from the rain, particularly when walking on the rock surface.

Ben said, "Wait here. Let me find the opening and we'll check out the biggest cave."

As Dave looked around excited to see the crater, Ben tentatively traversed the huge boulders along the rock face that formed the summit. Slipping and sliding on the glazed surfaces, his feet suddenly came out from under him and he smashed his head on an outcropping. His momentum carried him across the rock ledge, and he plunged down into one of the caverns.

Dave let out a primal scream, not believing what he had just seen. He sat there immobilized, trying to overcome the shock. Then, getting down on all fours, he crawled to where Ben had disappeared. He saw blood on the rock where his head hit and, as he peered over the edge of the fissure, he saw his father's motionless body lying at the bottom of the deep, gloomy cave in a foot of snow that was rapidly turning red. Realizing he could not climb down into the mammoth cave and trying to control his panic, Dave began sobbing. He lay on the frozen rock surface trembling, not knowing what to do. His only thought was, *I've got to help my dad.*

CHAPTER 23

Recovery

D AVE WAS SITTING on a threadbare couch in LeRoy's tiny cabin, which was actually a converted mobile home. LeRoy was on the phone with the State Police who serviced the town in the absence of a local police department. As he hung up, he and Dave both heard the siren wailing, alerting the volunteer fire and ambulance teams of an emergency.

Getting into LeRoy's truck, Dave was still badly shaken from seeing his father fall into the abyss. As they drove back to the Chimney Mountain base lot, he provided more detail about how the accident happened.

"When I saw him lying in the blood-covered snow, I slid back from the edge. I realized there was no way I could climb down there. I had to ease back where it was safe to stand. It was so hard leaving him there."

"You did the right thing, or otherwise there'd be two bodies at the bottom of that cavern. It was important to come back and get help."

"It's so icy up there, it took me nearly two hours to get down to the Jeep. I kept sliding and falling. I didn't know where to get help. I don't even remember driving to your house."

As they pulled into the parking area, they found two State Police cars there with lights flashing. They could hear the sirens coming up the road behind them. A car pulled in first. It was the fire chief. LeRoy introduced him to Dave.

"Hi, I'm Chief Warren. Tell me what happened up there."

Dave quickly related the experience and started to break down before he could finish.

As the fire trucks and ambulance arrived, the chief barked orders and told his men what equipment to bring. Wearing headlamps and carrying portable lights, ladders, and rope, they charged up the hill toward the summit. Dave and LeRoy followed but struggled to keep up, even without carrying equipment.

When they reached the summit, the rescue team had lights set up and were spreading sand around the area. They asked Dave to show them exactly where his dad had fallen. Shining lights down into the cave, they saw Ben's motionless body. The chief gave orders for the recovery.

Two men trained for this type of rescue were slowly lowered down to the floor of the cave on rope slings. When they got to Ben, they checked his vitals to no avail. He had no doubt died on impact, and his body was already partially frozen.

The team lowered a stretcher down and Ben's body was placed on it and secured. As the stretcher was raised, the two climbers waited to be brought back through the aperture. During the entire recovery operation, Dave sat on a log, rocking back and forth still in shock, and scared beyond belief. LeRoy kept coming over and comforting him.

Back in the parking area, a trooper with a clipboard took Dave's information and a brief statement. Up at the summit, his partner had taken photos of the bloodstained rock where Ben had hit is head. He also photographed the bottom of the cave.

The ambulance brought the body to the funeral home in town, and the volunteers drove the trucks back to the firehouse and returned home. LeRoy took Dave to his home on Cedar River and had a couple of volunteers go to his place and drive the Jeep to the Powers cabin.

Dave sat on his bed, and as the shock began to dissipate, he started crying again. It was the same feeling he had when his mother died. He felt abandoned and frightened. Only this time it was worse. His father wasn't there to protect him. He didn't know how he could survive alone in this wilderness, or anywhere else for that matter. *I am so screwed. What am I going to do?*

After crying himself to sleep fully clothed atop his comforter, he awoke in the middle of the night and began to assess his predicament. *Starting today, I have to be a man. I have to make the decisions to survive. What would Dad do if it happened to him?*

Pulling the comforter over him, he fell back asleep and awoke at sun-up. After making breakfast, he mimicked his father and made a list of tasks to undertake. His first one would be to call Rich Guerrero.

CHAPTER 24

Out of Isolation

THE BRIEF BURIAL SERVICE was held at the local cemetery and led by the funeral director. LeRoy and a few of the merchants and contractors in town who had gotten to know Ben and Dave attended. A group of young volunteer firemen also were on hand, having been moved by Dave's anguish on the mountaintop.

After the service, they invited him to join them at a local bar on Friday night. He was heartened by the gesture, as he was feeling desolate and alone without any friends.

Back at the cabin, he thought about his decision not to have a church service or have the pastor at the cemetery. It was contrary to his Catholic upbringing. But he was angry with his religion and the church. He felt that he was being punished by having his parents taken from him. *I'm going to prove I can take care of myself.*

Dave spent the rest of the day thinking about his list and what he had to do to survive on his own and live a fulfilling life in the mountains. Surprisingly, there was a substantial amount of money in the bank account in the Bahamas, much more than he expected. He later learned that the more than two million dollars included his father's inheritance and the insurance from his grandparents' deaths before he was born. Dave was gratified to learn the amount, but he felt he had to earn his own way and use that money for backup and supplemental income as he learned how to be productive.

When he called Rich Guerrero and told him about his father's tragic death, he also shared his decision to start supporting himself and become independent. Guerrero admired his maturity and encouraged his decision to earn a living. He asked Dave what help he needed immediately.

"Mr. Guerrero, right now I'm okay. When I figure out what I want to do and make a long-term plan, I'd like your advice on it."

"First, call me Rich. And when you think you have it figured out, let's discuss it. Please call anytime. I am indebted to your father, and I welcome the opportunity to repay what he did for my bank. Remember, I'm here to help."

Dave went into town to Marty's bar on Friday after he had an early dinner. As he walked in, he recognized some of the firemen gathered at the bar and they invited him to join them. It was about seven o'clock, and they had already been there a couple of hours. Ted Spring introduced himself and bought Dave a beer. He explained that he was LeRoy's cousin. The group toasted Dave and welcomed him to the mountains.

LeRoy, who was seated at a table in the back with a couple of older men, came over to Dave. "Well, I see you decided to give up the hermit life and join the guys for a drink."

"Hi, Roy. Yes, I was feeling isolated even before dad died. I need to be with some people my age."

"By golly, then get back to it with those young fellers at the bar."

Nursing his second beer, Dave asked Ted what he did for a living.

"I build Adirondack guide boats." Seeing his questioning look, he explained, "They are hand-crafted boats somewhere between a canoe and a rowboat. They're a heavier version of a canoe with oarlocks, so you row them rather than paddle them. Stop by my shop tomorrow and I'll show them to you."

Dave was impressed with the concept of this unusual boat made here in town by hand. He told Ted he would visit the shop the next day.

Discussing employment with the others in the group, Dave learned most of them worked for the state as road maintenance workers, and others were linemen with the utility company.

Lying in bed that night, Dave thought about the prospects of how he could earn a living. Although he hadn't completed high school, he was convinced his education was far superior to the level of the men he met that night. He decided to get a GED diploma and then see about some courses at the community college.

But education wasn't the issue. It wasn't going to get him where he felt he wanted to be. *I want to learn more about business, but a college degree isn't going to advance my career in the Adirondack Park.*

Earlier, he had looked around the bar. These were good men, satisfied with their jobs and their simple family life. Dave could not see himself in that role. There was no way he was going to work for an impersonal bureaucracy like the state. He could only envision being self-employed. The fireworks caper ensured that. *I'll focus on a business I can launch here and be successful.*

CHAPTER 25

A New Hobby

O N HIS WAY into town the next day, Dave stopped at Ted Spring's house. It was a small single-story white home with frame construction and plank siding. The house was only slightly larger than his cabin.

A couple of inches shy of six feet, Ted was about Dave's height but solidly built. He had a square face and a perpetual smile. His thinning brown hair made him look older than his thirty-five years.

Inside the shop, which was in a separate building of about 1,000 square feet, the open floor plan housed one finished boat and two or three in various stages of construction. Dave was impressed by the beauty and workmanship of these sleek boats. He thought, *These are artistic wood sculptures.* Ted beamed at Dave's reaction to his precision craftsmanship.

Dave asked how much they cost, and Ted answered, "They start at nearly $1,000 and go to about $3,000, depending on size and other factors. And they are guaranteed for life."

"Who can afford to buy these?"

"My customers are wealthy sportsmen who visit the area."

"But that's a small pool of customers. How do you survive?"

"Oh, I do fine. The income is all labor with virtually no overhead. It's a low-key lifestyle, and I really like what I do."

While Dave would love to own one, there was no way he could justify spending money on an extravagance like that. Inspired by

Ted, he left the shop with a new perspective. *Here's an entrepreneur, enjoying his craft and living in paradise. There's no reason why I can't be doing something similar.*

Later Dave went to the drugstore in town to buy some toiletries. He saw Kodak cameras on sale and, on impulse, he bought one along with three rolls of film. He had been awed by the magnificent sunsets over the mountains and he wanted to have some photos of them. The druggist told him that he could have his film developed at the store in 24 hours.

Dave spent the next few days taking pictures of the small islands in the lakes, some wildlife photos, and other scenes that he encountered. He brought the film in for processing and was anxious to see the results.

The snapshots he got back included a few beautiful photos, but most were mediocre. Disappointed, he went to the library to borrow a book on photography. He noted that the single-story building was a fraction of the enormous library at LaSalle, but he was pleasantly surprised by the range of topics available from its inventory. The librarian, Mrs. Stanton, looked at his photos and encouraged him, saying, "I see some promise in your framing and staging of the subjects."

She recommended he do more experimenting and read a couple of books she suggested to help him improve his results. She also showed him a few photos hanging in the library that she had taken. He said, "These are amazing. I want my photos to look like this." The compliment delighted the middle-aged woman.

After reading and absorbing both books, Dave went out and took some more photos, including a few sunset shots. When the developed pictures came in, he rushed over to the library and showed them to Mrs. Stanton. They both saw the improvement, but Dave was still disappointed in the results.

She said, "Now these are really good compositions. Just compare them to your first attempts at photography."

"But the quality of the pictures is poor, and there is no depth of field on the close-ups of the flowers. The books talked about that a lot."

"If you want professional quality, you need to get a professional camera, and you need to use a professional lab to process your prints. A drugstore processor is okay to develop the film, but they can't deliver high-quality, custom prints."

She then told him about a lab in Albany that made her prints. She also suggested he buy a single-lens reflex camera, preferably a Nikon, and a few different lenses.

Dave searched the Yellow Pages and found a few camera shops that were all in Albany, and the following week he took the three-hour drive down to the city. One of the shops he visited was a retail store with a huge selection of cameras, lenses, and accessories. The proprietor, who was knowledgeable in photography, made excellent recommendations and even advised against buying certain items.

Dave spent over $500 on his purchases. He now had a Nikon body, several lenses including a zoom and a telephoto, a tripod, a light meter, a camera case, and a handful of filters.

Before leaving Albany, Dave found the processing lab Mrs. Stanton had recommended. Walking into the office at the front of the small commercial building, his nostrils were assaulted by the smell of the chemicals used for developing and printing. He introduced himself to the owner, and they had a great conversation. Dave told him that as his work improved, he'd be sending down negatives for making enlargements.

Driving back, Dave was excited about the photography he was going to produce with his professional equipment. But he had no idea how it was about to change his life.

CHAPTER 26

The Hobby Becomes a Passion

WITHIN WEEKS, Dave was producing professional-quality photography, often showing the best results to Mrs. Stanton. She enthusiastically encouraged him, "These get better every week. Keep doing more and expand your subjects."

Her praise propelled him and gave him the idea to have a few of his best photos enlarged and mounted to heavyweight chipboard. He planned to decorate his drab cabin with them.

When the mounted prints arrived, they looked so impressive they gave him an idea. He brought the finished pieces to the general store and showed them to Gibby. He asked, "Do you think your tourist customers would buy these?"

Gibby was as impressed as Mrs. Stanton and immediately became interested in selling them, not just to the tourists who frequented the store, but also to some of the locals to hang in their homes. They agreed on pricing, and Dave began to produce hundreds of mounted photos in several sizes. As the sales began to grow, so did his encouragement to expand his outlets. He brought samples to shops in all the surrounding towns, adding to his distribution channel.

As his photography became popular, Dave began signing each photo, which enabled him to increase the perceived value and the price. He also bought quantities of frames from a manufacturer and started distributing framed prints as well as mounted ones.

To expand his small business, he created a flyer with some of the most popular photos and had the lab produce 20 copies. He then looked up stores that catered to tourists in the larger towns in the Adirondacks and mailed them. Twelve of the stores agreed to carry his photo prints. He printed more flyers, researched stores in other parts of the state, and did more mailings. His mini advertising campaign was working better than expected.

Mrs. Stanton suggested to Dave that he drive up to the Adirondack Museum and show the curator his photography. The multi-building museum located in the next town was on a landscaped campus with spectacular views overlooking Blue Mountain Lake. It was a stunning facility.

The entire staff was impressed with the photos Dave had in his portfolio and they made several recommendations.

The curator said, "First of all, there's a bulletin board in the lobby where you can hang one of your flyers. Our visitors would welcome the opportunity to access your work." She also told him that the museum would purchase enlarged prints from time to time, as their displays were updated. And she suggested he participate in some of the photo contests that were held in the mountains. He returned home encouraged to continue and expand his passion which was now a growing business.

On the way back to his cabin, Dave had another idea. Thinking about the beauty of the museum's campus, he decided to return and take photos of the buildings, and the beautiful grounds that sloped down to the pristine lake. He would then offer enlarged prints to the museum to sell in their gift shop.

Dave got a call from Ted one morning inviting him to take a ride in a new Adirondack Guide Boat. He said, "I'm taking my newest boat for a test run on Indian Lake. Why don't you join me?"

Dave was ecstatic at the offer. "I would love that! I want to learn how these boats handle compared to rowboats or canoes."

They spent the morning cruising the small islands in the lake, and Dave took dozens of photos. At one point, they switched seats and Dave rowed. He was impressed by how easy it was to row this design compared to a standard rowboat.

When they got back to shore, Dave took some photos of the boat, including a few with Ted rowing. They stopped for lunch at Joe's Luncheonette in town and Dave again asked about how Ted was able to get enough customers for such an expensive boat.

"The tourists who visit here have varying incomes. There are a lot of blue-collar workers who come up to hunt or bring their families for a wilderness vacation. But there are also a lot of very wealthy people who have vacation homes on the lakes, and some hidden away in the woods. The Sutrinas, for instance. They have a huge house on 200 acres that sits a mile in from the road. No one except us locals even knows it's there."

"It still sounds like a small pool of customers to draw from."

"I agree, but I can keep busy enough to make a living. And I love working with wood."

"I get that. I feel the same way about this photography business I started. It's great to make money while you're having fun."

Dave got the film from their boat cruise processed, and when he saw the prints it gave him an idea. He sat at the table with the photos of Ted's boat and he wrote an ad concept.

Excited, he drove over to Ted's shop and showed him the ad layout. "I have a way for you to increase your business. Sooner or later, you will build a boat for everyone in town who wants to spend the money to own one. But why not let people in some of the more populated and affluent Adirondack towns know about your boats. Like Lake Placid and Lake George?"

"How can I do that? I don't have any money to advertise."

"Neither do I. But I started promoting my business on a shoestring and it's growing like crazy.

"Let's run an ad in just one small town. If you get an order, you can spend a little more money on ads in other towns, until you are at capacity. You may even be able to hire and train an assistant to help you."

Intrigued by the idea, Ted decided to test the ad concept. The first ad that Ted ran in a small Lake Saranac newspaper enabled him to sell two boats.

Recognizing the opportunity, Ted began to search for an apprentice, knowing that even with taking the time to train a new employee, the hired hand would relieve him from countless hours of the more tedious parts of the construction process. If it worked out, he could then train a second apprentice.

Seeing Ted's success, Dave decided to take his own advice and hire someone to help with the mounting and framing of the enlarged photos. He also needed a shop to warehouse his inventory and expand the framing and shipping operation. He hired a contractor and began construction on a building similar to Ted's, as he searched for the right candidate to bring on board.

CHAPTER 27

A New Friend

A YEAR PASSED after Dave's foray into advertising his photography and Ted's boat business. During that time, word got around about his success at creating marketing messages that got results.

He produced an ad and a mailer for a plumbing contractor promoting a home-watch service for people who owned vacation homes in the Adirondacks. He also did ads for a few other services based in town. Some of the locals resented his advertising work. They felt it was unfair, and that sales should come from word of mouth and reputation. Dave could not understand this Neanderthal thinking. *The ads are working, and they must be jealous.*

As his reputation spread, he attracted bigger clients located in some of the larger towns like Glens Falls and Lake George, where he produced advertising for a few tourist attractions and a large restaurant. His advertising concepts were producing excellent results because the message appealed to the target audience. They didn't just make the reader aware of the product or service. They emphasized the benefits and entertained the reader as they sold the product.

Dave's unusual approach to his ad concepts was what set them apart from the other ads in the newspapers and magazines. He almost always included his dramatic photography and his sense of humor. These features got people's attention, making them interested in reading his ads.

The advertising business was dominating his schedule and generating substantial income. But he didn't want to give up the photography business. Fortunately, the intern he hired, Bill Perry, was doing an excellent job of managing and processing the orders. Bill was an art major at Adirondack Community College and an excellent photographer himself. Dave began adding some of Bill's photography to his offerings catalog, paying him a royalty on prints sold.

By Friday evening, Dave was ready for a break from the business. He often went to the bar for a few beers and commiserated with the guys. He usually got there at about six or seven o'clock, and by then many of the younger guys were already well along in their quest to get drunk.

The men in Indian Lake were so different from Dave. They grew up poor and their lives were the product of the harsh elements of the mountain wilderness. Their education was limited, in many cases including nothing more than grammar school or a year or two of high school.

These men took jobs anywhere they could get one and married from the available pool of girls in town. They lived simple lives with no aspirations to go beyond their current circumstances. It was difficult, but they were not unhappy.

The men greeted Dave as he came in. He was one of the only full-time residents who did not grow up in the area. Most of them liked him, as he was an anomaly. And they enjoyed hearing his stories of growing up in a big city.

Unfortunately, one of the regulars, Johnny Savorie, despised Dave. He was a malcontent and resented anyone who was successful, or that he perceived to come from a privileged background. Johnny had trouble holding his liquor, his job, and his temper. Dave always tried to avoid him as he knew he would be baited into an argument with this borderline psychopathic alcoholic.

As Dave was finishing his first beer, a well-dressed guy came in and sat next to him and said, "You must be the photography guy?"

"Yes, I am. Hi. And you are?"

"I'm Robbie Sutrina. I saw some of your work at Gibby's, and he showed me an ad you did for Ted Spring. It's very good work, especially up here."

"Thanks, I appreciate it."

"Let me buy you a beer."

The name registered from Ted's comment about the Sutrina estate. Extending his hand he said, "I'm Dave Powers. Glad to meet you."

When Robbie put a $100 bill on the bar to pay for the beers, Savorie shouted, "Look, guys. The fucking millionaire is paying for his beer with a hundred-dollar bill! That's more than we make in a week. And this prick probably never worked a day in his life."

Robbie answered, "Bartender, Buy Johnny a beer."

"Fuck you, Sutrina. I don't need your charity. I got a new job, and I can pay for my own drinks."

Ignoring the comment, Robbie began talking to Dave and they got into a long conversation. Robbie, who was only three years older than Dave, told him he worked for his father's printing company in New York City. His clients were all the big advertising agencies and some of the national magazine publishers based in the city.

Looking around, he confided, "They think I'm spending my father's money, but I make big bucks at the firm. And my wife is loaded."

Dave answered, "I now do advertising, and the business is growing rapidly. But I don't handle much printing, just an occasional flyer."

"If you ever get any big printing projects, you call me. I'll give you a good deal so you can add a markup."

Being ignored by just about everyone, Savorie again tried to insert himself into Robbie and Dave's conversation. "Look at the two faggots having a little love fest. Nobody else will talk to them, so they got each other."

Ted Spring, who was sitting at a table with a few friends answered,

"Johnny, shut your ass. No one wants to listen to you when you're drunk. Just go home and sleep it off."

Savorie jumped off his barstool, knocking it over, "I'll kick your fuckin' ass, Spring."

Before he could turn around, the bartender grabbed him and pushed him out the front door. "Savorie, if you don't start behaving in here, I'm going to throw you out for good. Everybody's tired of your shit."

With that, Robbie said to Dave, "I've got to get to the house, but I'm coming over to your place tomorrow. I want to see your work. You're out by the Cedar River flow, right?"

"Yes, at the end of the dirt road. I'll be around all morning and doing some photography in the late afternoon. I'll look forward to seeing you."

CHAPTER 28

Meeting the Sutrinas

WHEN ROBBIE SHOWED up the next morning, Dave took him into the shop and showed him his setup. The business operation was run from a small office in the front of the building. Hanging on the walls were enlargements of all the ads he had created. And in the back room, with its work counter and storage shelves, Dave had displayed dozens of his photographs.

Robbie had seen some of Dave's photography at the general store, but he was shocked at the quality of the advertising. "Dave, this is as good as anything I've seen in New York. I could get you business in the city. Would you be willing to drive down?"

"Not really. I've got enough to keep me busy up here. Why spend all day driving to the city to get work?"

"It pays better, that's why. You could make a fortune."

"That's not what I'm looking for. I'm living the dream. My business is growing nicely and I'm having fun. I make enough to be comfortable and then some. But hey, I appreciate your offer. I do."

"That does sound special. But there's nothing like making a ton of money. So, do you hunt? We've got prime deer hunting land at my place."

"I haven't yet, but I would use a bow instead of a rifle. I'm an excellent archer."

"The problem is you can't get close enough with a bow. These deer are very wary in the winter, just like the turkeys."

"Oh, I think I can take one down from a distance, but I'd love to try it and find out."

"Why don't you come over to my place tomorrow? We'll do some shooting and have dinner with my family."

When Robbie left, Dave thought about how he described his life to him. *After losing both my parents, I'm so fortunate to have landed on my feet and live this carefree lifestyle, making money from hobbies I love.*

The next day, Dave drove to the Sutrina estate a couple of miles south of the village. He nearly missed the entrance to the property, which was a non-descript dirt driveway with a light covering of crushed stone. As he drove the mile-long dirt track up and down the hills, he came to a crest in the road and was struck by the immense fieldstone house sitting atop the next hill with a huge grass pasture in front of it. The field was covered with tall grasses and wildflowers.

As he pulled up, Robbie came out and greeted him. "So, what do you think?"

Dave looked around in awe. "The view is amazing." On his right was a pine forest that stretched for miles, and across the valley rose a mountain that towered over the surrounding peaks.

They went into the house where Robbie introduced his parents, Katie and Papa Joe, and his kid brother, Luke. A tall, full-figured woman with blonde hair and blue eyes, Katie embraced Dave in a warm hug. Papa Joe asked how long he'd lived in town. Ruggedly handsome with chiseled features, his olive complexion, brown eyes, and sharp nose showed his Italian heritage. Both parents were very cordial, making Dave feel at home.

Walking through the house, Robbie explained that all the building materials came from the property and took a year to collect. The sunken living room was dominated by a massive stone fireplace, with a trophy stag head mounted over the mantle. All the walls were varnished knotty pine, giving the entire house the feel of the wilderness. Even the trestle table and benches in the dining room were the same pine.

After coffee, Robbie said, "Okay, let's do some shooting. Luke, you want to join us?"

"No thanks, Robbie. I've got some things to do."

Taking two rifles from the gun cabinet, they went out back behind the barn. There was a shooting area set up in front of a steep hill with some targets plus miscellaneous cans and bottles. Before they began shooting, Dave asked Robbie, "Doesn't Luke like to shoot?"

"No. All he does is listen to his music and read."

Robbie then began to explain gun safety to Dave, who interrupted. "I went to military school, and I'm proficient at handling firearms. But as I said, I prefer archery."

"Then, let's do both."

Robbie was somewhat better with a rifle than Dave, but didn't come close to Dave's ability with a bow. Even at long distances, Dave consistently hit the bullseye. Robbie complimented him, saying, "You are a marksman with that bow. You're going to have to shoot a buck with that thing, so you have camp meat for the winter."

"I've never eaten wild game. What's it taste like?"

"Bear tastes like shit, but venison is the best-tasting meat you will ever eat. I'll give you a couple of steaks to take home. After you have it, you'll be out in the woods getting your own buck."

For dinner that night, Papa Joe served a small wild turkey and a few partridges from the property. For Dave, these were all new taste sensations. The turkey his mom made for Thanksgiving never had a flavor close to this.

When he left, Katie told him, "Don't be a stranger. Stop in anytime."

Papa Joe suggested he visit their printing plant when he came to

New York. Robbie shook his hand and said, "I'll let you know when I'm coming back up. We'll do some hunting."

Driving back to his camp, Dave thought, *I can't believe how genuinely warm and friendly these people are. They are not typical New Yorkers. I can see Robbie and me becoming close friends.*

CHAPTER 29

Mob Justice

DAVE READ ABOUT an Indian Festival being held in Lake George. Descendants of all the major upstate tribes would be on hand. One of the events which caught his attention was an archery contest. He drove down for the Sunday contest to compete.

Dozens of contestants had signed up, most of them proudly wearing their native garb. The elimination tournament took nearly three hours to complete, and in the end, Dave had scored the best in every round and was declared the winner.

Afterward, Dave was interviewed by a journalist for a story in the regional newspaper. A newcomer to the Adirondacks beating out all the locals and native Americans made big news.

When Dave walked into the bar the following Friday night, he was greeted with cheers from just about everyone there. The bartender bought Dave a beer, and all the men toasted his success at the archery competition.

But Johnny Savorie wasn't cheering. He shouted down the bar, "Hey, the faggot is an Indian now. Let's see you do a war dance, faggot."

"Why don't you quiet down and nurse your beer?" Dave said. "No one wants to listen to you."

Rushing down to where Dave sat, Johnny got in his face. "C'mon.

We're going outside and I'm going to clean the parking lot with your ugly puss."

Before Johnny could say another word, Ted Spring grabbed him and pushed him out the door and down the steps where he lay on the ground, face down. "Savorie, go sleep it off in your truck and then go home. Everyone is tired of your mouth."

Getting up and brushing himself off, Savorie staggered into the parking lot fuming. Deciding to mess up their vehicles, he picked up a rock to smash the Jeep's windshield but stopped when he saw Dave's bow on the back seat. He grabbed it and a few arrows and waited in his truck.

Dave bought Ted a beer and they sat and talked together. "Thanks for stepping in, but you didn't have to. I can handle that punk."

"It's okay. I've been looking for the chance to knock the little bastard on his ass. It felt good."

They finished a couple of beers and left together. Saying good night, Dave jumped in his Jeep and drove toward home, while Ted walked to his truck in the back of the lot. As he was climbing into the cab, Johnny came up behind him and shot an arrow at close range into his back.

The arrow's razor tip went between two ribs and pierced Ted's lung. He slumped forward, hit his head on the running board, and lay face down unconscious in the dirt. Savorie tossed the bow and extra arrows on the ground alongside the building. He ran back into the bar yelling, "Powers just shot Ted with an arrow! They were arguing. I saw the whole thing."

Ted was one of the best-liked men in town and everyone ran out of the bar in disbelief. One of the firemen checked his pulse, which was very weak, and he shouted for someone to call for an ambulance. Savorie yelled, "That chicken-shit bastard! Let's go get the fucker."

CHAPTER 30

A Safe Haven

SITTING IN HIS OFFICE, Dave heard a caravan of cars and trucks coming up his driveway. This concerned him as he rarely got visitors. He put out the light and waited in the dark. When he saw the out-of-control mob start burning his cabin down, he snuck out the back door and ran off.

After escaping the mob, Dave found himself past town on Route 28. He kept running away from Indian Lake and toward North Creek. He had no idea why the men in town turned against him. All he knew was he wasn't safe among the locals. He thought of going to LeRoy's, but he didn't know who he could trust. He came to the Sutrinas place and decided to run up their driveway. They were from out of town, and they had befriended him.

Seeing the lights still on, he knocked on the door. Katie answered, shocked to see him standing there covered in perspiration and dirt. "Dave, what's wrong? Are you okay? Please come in."

Hearing the commotion, Luke came running down the stairs. "Mom, what's going on?" Recognizing their visitor, he added, "Dave, what happened to you?"

They sat at the long dining room table and Dave told them what had transpired over the last few hours. "I stopped in town for a beer with the guys. I've been meeting them every few weeks. Johnny

Savorie started giving me a hard time, and Ted Spring came over and threw him out of the bar."

Luke commented, "Savorie is always drunk and looking for a fight."

"Yeah, I avoid him. Ted and I left together. And after I got home, a mob from town showed up and burned my camp and warehouse down, even my Jeep."

Katie was shocked. "Oh my God. How awful. How did you get away?"

"I slipped into the woods and made my way here. You're the only people I feel safe around right now."

The house had no phone, so Katie said, "Luke, go up to town and get LeRoy."

Dave stopped her. "Is he trustworthy? Will he be on their side? They want to kill me. I'm really scared."

"You don't have to worry about LeRoy. He's loyal to us, and he's the fairest man I've ever met. He'll know what's going on, and he'll tell you what to do."

Luke drove off, and Katie made coffee. She told Dave to use the bathroom and get cleaned up.

About a half-hour later Luke returned with LeRoy. He came running in the house and asked, "Dave, is it true you shot Ted with your bow?"

"What? Absolutely not! I would never hurt anyone. I think you know me better than that. Ted's my friend and a client."

"Then what did happen? Tell me everything."

LeRoy sat down as Katie put a cup of coffee in front of him. Dave reiterated everything he told Katie and Luke. LeRoy listened intently and asked, "Where was your bow before you left the bar?"

"It was in the back of my jeep. It's all open and anyone walking by could see it."

"Yup. That explains it. Only a spineless bully like Savorie would pull a stunt like that."

"You think Savorie shot Ted?"

Sipping his coffee, he answered, "Yup. He never liked Ted. 'Course, he never likes anybody. He's jealous of your success being here such a short time and makin' friends with the men in town. And he probably was drunk enough to do it."

"He was drunk and nasty like always. But I never thought he had it in him to do in his neighbor."

"Dave, this is rough country, and we live hard lives here. But we can't sit here talkin' 'bout it. When they realize you didn't burn up in that fire, they'll come lookin' for ya. And they're gonna be a lynch mob, for sure. We gotta get you outta here right away."

LeRoy suggested that Luke drive Dave down to Sutrina's house in New Jersey until an investigation was held and Dave could be cleared. He said, "You two should leave now and take turns drivin'. I'm gonna talk to Captain Truesdale from the State Police. We do some huntin' together. It'll help move the investigation along."

He turned to Katie. "Since you only have one car here, I'll drive you around 'til Luke gets back."

As the two men prepared to leave, Katie hugged Dave and asked, "Do you need some money?"

"Thank you, no. I have some cash and a credit card. I'll be fine."

Leroy then left and headed uptown. There was one thing he needed to check out right away.

CHAPTER 31

Escape from Paradise

LUKE AND DAVE drove through the night, alternating at the wheel and taking naps. They stopped for breakfast in Nyack. They hadn't talked much in the car, as they each took advantage of the time to catch some sleep. In the coffee shop, Luke became more animated and talked about the country music he liked. He was a tall lanky kid who always had a smirk on his face. He had his mother's coloring and dressed like a cowboy, western boots and all. *No surprise there.*

Luke called his brother Robbie to tell him he'd be home in about an hour. He had Dave Powers with him as there was trouble in Indian Lake. Robbie told him he was just having breakfast with his wife, and he'd meet them at the house.

When they got to their impressive Englewood Cliffs neighborhood, Luke pulled into the circular driveway of a stately white, front-to-back split-level house. With a two-car garage on the side, the structure was surrounded by mature trees and lush landscaping.

After Robbie arrived, Dave retold what had happened both at the bar and at his house.

Robbie started cursing and concluded, "Savorie is behind this, for sure. He acts like a bully, but he's a chicken-shit bastard. I can't believe he had the balls to kill Ted. Everybody loves Ted."

"I don't know what happened after I left, but LeRoy told us that he was shot in the back with an arrow. So it points to me. Who else uses a bow up there?"

"That makes it look bad for you. And I don't know how you're going to beat their mountain justice. They tend to stick together. Regardless of what happens, you can't live there anymore. They burned you out, and there's nothing to go back to."

"What am I going to do? It's where I live and where I work. Both the photography business and the advertising services are doing great."

"First, we've got to keep you out of jail. Even if you beat this, your business is toast. All you have now is some land. Let it go."

"You mean sell it?"

"Nah, it isn't worth anything. I'll get you a job in the city. You've got a great creative mind, and New York is hungry for talent like yours."

"Robbie, I have nothing. All the ad work I produced is in an ash heap. The only thing I can recover is the photography. The lab has negatives on all my work."

"I have an idea." Handing his business card to Dave, he continued, "Call the lab and have them make 10x14 prints of your best photos and have them sent to my office."

And thinking for a minute, he added, "And make a list of newspapers and magazines where your ads ran. I'll get someone in the office to call them and see if they can send out copies of the ads. We'll make a portfolio and I'll set up appointments to present your work to some ad agencies."

Luke interrupted them, saying, "You guys make your plans. I'm going upstairs and get some sleep. And then I'm driving back up to the lake. Dave, I'll call you here tomorrow and let you know what LeRoy finds out."

Robbie then said to Dave, "Putting a portfolio together and getting you some interviews is going to take some time. I'll talk to my dad. You can come to work at the printing company in the meantime. It will be good experience."

"I don't want to impose on your family."

Robbie continued, "Not a problem. Dave, after you call the lab, take my old bedroom. It's the first one upstairs. Rest up and then go buy some clothes and a new suit. My dad's driving the Corvette, so take the caddy in the garage."

"This is all too much. I'll be okay."

"Bullshit. I'll see if I can get you a car to use until you get on your feet. See you tonight when I get back from the city."

※　※　※

While Dave and Luke had been driving down from the mountains, LeRoy went back uptown. He parked in the lot next to the bar, which was now empty. Taking out his flashlight, he began walking the perimeter.

In minutes he found Dave's bow along with a few arrows. Taking out a bandana, he picked them up and put them in his truck. He then went home and called Captain Truesdale.

In the morning, Truesdale came by. LeRoy offered him a cup of coffee and showed him what he found in the parking lot. "I know I'm not s'posed to interfere with a crime scene, but if I left it there, someone with wrong intentions woulda taken it. I'll betcha anythin' Johnny Savorie's fingerprints are on that bow."

PART III

Back to Civilization?

CHAPTER 32

A Temporary Fix

Despite the terror-filled previous night with nearly no sleep, Dave spent a few fitful hours laying on Robbie's bed without dozing off. He couldn't wrap his head around what had happened to the fulfilling life he was building in Indian Lake.

After my dad died, I was so lucky to find a way to support myself doing stuff I liked, and then I had to run away. It's all gone.

Now he lay in a strange bed, a fugitive from his beloved home. *Can I go back to New York City with this fake identity and have a life like I just lost?*

It was 11 in the morning when the phone rang, and Dave was the only one in Papa Joe's house. Now in the kitchen having coffee, he jumped up and grabbed the turquoise wall phone. "This is Dave."

"Dave, it's Robbie. When I got to the office I spoke to my dad. He wants you to come in with him tomorrow and start working in the production office. Carlo will train you, and you can work here as long as you want."

"Robbie, this is all moving so fast. I don't know what to say."

"Look, I'm still going to create a portfolio for you. You have too much talent for the printing business, but the knowledge is good. Now, go buy some clothes."

When Papa Joe got home that night, it was after seven. He came in and greeted Dave, "Nice to see you again, kid. I just wish it were under better circumstances. Did you eat?"

"Hi, Papa Joe. I can't thank you and your family enough for helping me. I don't know what I would have done without you. And no, I haven't eaten."

"I'll get a pizza brought over. We'll have a beer while we're waiting."

Pulling two glass bottles from the refrigerator and handing one to Dave, he said "I'm glad you're coming to work for me, even if it's temporary. You'll learn the printing business, and who knows? Down the road, you may need to have printing done, and you'll know who to come to."

The next morning, the two men drove into the city. When they got to the plant, Dave was shocked at its size. About a dozen presses large and small were running and skids of paper were stacked everywhere. The cacophony of the presses and binding equipment was deafening.

Papa Joe brought Dave into the production department and introduced him to Carlo. "He will be your boss and will teach you all about printing."

Carlo was an imposing man, jovial and crude. He grew up in the Italian section of lower Manhattan, a few blocks from where Dave used to buy firecrackers. Carlo was medium height, with a huge belly, but moved around the shop like an athlete. Dave enjoyed being around him, listening to his colorful banter, laced with a constant barrage of expletives. Every sentence contained an F-bomb.

Settling into the job, Dave commuted with Papa Joe from Englewood Cliffs every day. He followed Carlo around the huge shop floor, learning all the steps to getting a printing project completed.

Remembering his mother's violent death, their hasty departure from the city, and his father's tale of revenge, Dave was apprehensive about being back in New York. His dad had warned him to never go back there again. It took him weeks to relax in this city of eight million people. Up until then, it was akin to the time he was selling the fireworks.

Robbie came running out of his office one morning. His mother had just called him from Indian Lake. "Dave, Dave! LeRoy just called my mom. Ted Spring is going to be okay. He's home recovering and will be back working in a few weeks."

"Wow, that's great! I'm so glad for him. He's a really good guy."

"And even better news—Johnnie Savorie pleaded guilty to attempted murder after they confirmed his fingerprints on the bow."

"So, I guess it's safe to go back to the lake. I do miss it."

"Dave, think about it. It will never be the same for you. You can visit sometime in the future, but you can never live there again. It's time to move on."

Dave reflecting on the situation. *Robbie's right. The chemistry has changed, but I will miss it.*

For the next few months, Dave absorbed all the details of the process, from plate making to printing to binding. It was far more complex than he had expected, but he learned how the company achieved its superior printing results.

The photos from the lab came in, and Robbie received copies of ads from several upstate publications. He bought a large portfolio case and put together an impressive presentation of Dave's work. Handing the portfolio to Dave, he said, "Now I'll get you some appointments."

While he enjoyed this education in print production, he recognized this wasn't where he wanted to spend his career. Dave kept hoping he'd get a call to present his work to an ad agency.

One morning Robbie came in and said to him, "I was out with some top brass from Dunlap Brice Brighton last night, and their production VP Jerry Wantah set up a meeting for you with one of the group creative directors. Her name is Elisa Orsini, but I don't know her. Write down this information."

Dave took the information and called her that day. Her assistant answered his call and set up an appointment for him at 4 p.m. the following Wednesday.

CHAPTER 33

The Interview

WEARING HIS NEW SUIT, Dave showed up 15 minutes early but was kept waiting until 4:40. Sitting in the large reception area crowded with visitors, he went over his presentation and thought about the answers to possible questions she would ask. He became intimidated with the other salespeople and visitors, all relaxed and confident as they waited to be called into their appointments.

As the waiting time continued, he conjured up images of what she looked like. He was hoping she was young and beautiful. As it got later, his impression drifted towards her being older, then more matronly and unattractive. Finally, he was convinced she was downright ugly.

When he was the only one left in the reception room, a young woman dressed like a teenager came out to retrieve him. She made no apology or explanation for the delay. All she said was, "Miss Orsini will see you now." She brought him into a small conference room and told him to have a seat, but never said another word. Fifteen more minutes passed, and Dave now pictured her looking like a witch. The hour-and-a-half waiting time had sapped his energy and enthusiasm and he was getting ready to leave.

The door then opened and two women rushed in, one being the teen wannabe in her drooping beehive hairstyle. The other woman, who was not much older, said, "Mr. Powers? I'm Elisa Orsini, and this

is my secretary, Tiffany. So, show me what you have, and let's talk."
She did not look like a witch but rather was quietly beautiful. She was
short and pert. Her large hazel eyes set in a round face contrasted with
her dark hair. But her best feature was her amazingly smooth, olive
skin. She was all business.

Summoning up his strength, he said, "Hi, ladies. Everyone calls
me Dave. I've been working up in the Adirondack Mountains, doing
successful ad campaigns for local businessmen up there." As he spoke,
he pulled out some mounted ads for his retail clients.

The two women began to giggle at the clients represented in
the ads, causing Dave to sag. Elisa said, "Don't you have any work
for national clients, or is it all local retail stuff? We don't handle
advertising for small retailers. Our clients are all national brands."

Quickly recovering, Dave answered, "I'm sorry, but there are no
national companies based in the Adirondacks."

"How can I consider you for a position here with that portfolio?
It's too amateurish."

"Hold on. I think you're being swayed by the size of the client,
rather than the creativity of the work. Instead of looking at the logos,
read the headlines and the copy. They are attention-grabbing and
they sell. And don't overlook the photography."

And with that, he pulled out an ad for the Adirondack Museum
with a large photo of a sunset over Blue Mountain Lake. "This was
taken on the museum property during fall foliage."

Both women were stopped in their tracks by the beauty of the
photo. Elisa said, "Who took this?"

"I took this and the photos in all the other ads I'm showing you.
I also wrote the copy for every one of them."

"Dave, do you have a TV reel or any radio?"

"No. I've only done print ads for my clients."

"Then how can I hire you? We do a lot of TV here."

"I'm looking around this conference room. I see lots of print ads.

And what are TV commercials? They're animated print ads. They start with storyboards. The creative concepts are the same."

"Okay, let me think about it. I need to hire more staff, but I'm not sure you're a good fit. I'll get back to you."

Knowing he was being blown off, and since he had nothing to lose, Dave said what was on his mind. "The ads I see around this room are all good, but none are better than the work I just showed you. You're being prejudiced by the size of my clients, not my creativity. It makes me wonder if you actually recognize good advertising when you see it. But thank you for your time."

Elisa stood up and curtly said, "Tiffany will walk you out."

As Dave was escorted to the reception desk, Elisa walked back to her office. She was thinking about the interview and Dave's comments. *He was right and had the courage to say it, but I can't take a chance on hiring him. I'm a woman in a man's world. It could jeopardize the position I worked so hard to attain.*

CHAPTER 34

Using the Back Door

ROBBIE CALLED HIM on the weekend and asked how the presentation went. "She rejected my portfolio. It's all local retail."

"But, Dave, it doesn't matter. It's good work."

"I know, and I told her that. She was a real hard-ass and too insecure to hire me."

"My wife and I are having dinner in the city tonight. Meet us at Gallagher's at seven and bring your portfolio. I have an idea."

Dave got to the restaurant ten minutes after Robbie and his wife, Shelly. She was rail-thin, which made her long face look less attractive. Her bleached blonde hair and heavily applied makeup helped her appearance at first glance, but close up her face looked painted. They were both drinking martinis as Dave ordered a bottle of Budweiser.

Robbie took the portfolio and began to page through it, showing the ads to Shelly. She was mostly bored but was attracted to the photography of a few ads. She tittered at how the photos played off the humor in the headlines. She said, "These are very good. Did you take the pictures?"

Robbie answered, "Dave's photography is special. He has a great eye for composing a shot."

And to Dave, "I'm going to take a few of these ads to Jerry Wantah and show him your creativity. Now, let's order dinner."

The men ordered ribeye steaks. Shelly selected the filet mignon and asked for another martini. The steaks were huge, but they both ate every scrap of meat on the large bone. Shelly picked at her dinner, leaving most of it. She then had a third martini.

When the plates were cleared, Robbie told Dave about some of his other clients and the type of printing he did. He also reassured Dave that Wantah would respond well to the ads and would push Elisa Orsini.

Dave was pleased that Robbie was going the extra mile for him, but he knew it was a waste of time with her. "You may need to find another agency that would be more receptive to my work. She's a dead end."

"Maybe, but I'll try him one more time and then move on."

CHAPTER 35

The Assignment

TIFFANY CALLED DAVE on Tuesday and told him Elisa would like to meet in the next day or two to discuss an assignment. He said he could be there Thursday morning.

When he arrived, Tiffany came out to the reception desk and brought him into the same conference room. She handed him a strategy sheet for a campaign to promote tourism for a new Caribbean Island client. She said, "Read this and Elisa will be in shortly to discuss it with you."

As she left the room, Dave began reading the report. The goal of the campaign was to create awareness of the tourist amenities and stunning natural beauty of the island. The secondary goal was to attract affluent visitors to this new vacation destination.

Elisa walked in and before sitting down she said, "Apparently you have friends in high places here."

"Actually, I don't. My friend Robbie is a vendor here and works with some of the top executives."

"Well, it's not the best way to start out with any company. You look for a job based on your merits, not because you know someone."

"Look, Elisa, this wasn't my idea. I have the skills, but I didn't ask to be brought back in. I get that you can't risk hiring me."

"You're here because I was told to give you a chance to see what you could do."

"You weren't going to hire me when I first came in. And it sounds like you're not going to hire me now. You're not strong enough to bring me on. I get that, so why are we wasting each other's time?

"Jerry Wantah asked me to see what you could come up with for a national client. I'm not hiring you. I'm offering you a freelance assignment. I will pay you $250 to develop a concept for a TV commercial for this tourism client."

"And if I come up with a good storyboard, what then? How do I get past this adversarial block between us?"

"You probably can't. I'm working on this project myself, and I have an excellent concept that I'm completing. But look at it this way. You're getting $250 to create a storyboard that you can use to get a job at a smaller ad agency. So, take the assignment and let me get back to work."

Dave left the building disappointed with Elisa's attitude but pleased with the consolation prize. It convinced him that he would have to start out seeking employment with smaller agencies. He would call Robbie and explain that to him. Maybe he had a contact at one of the small or mid-size agencies or design studios.

In the meantime, he would work on this assignment and see what he could create. *I would love to come up with a better concept than hers, not that it would change anything.*

CHAPTER 36

Dazzling Demonstration

DAVE PLUNGED into the project and quickly came up with a terrific idea. But knowing a storyboard could not convey his concept, he would have to find a different way to present it. He called his friend Rich Guerrero at the Bahamas Bank and asked him if he could quickly assemble about a dozen photos of island scenes, including beaches, palm trees, plus tourist activities, like scuba diving, nighttime entertainment, etc., and airmail them to him right away.

That same day, Dave went to a stock photography firm and selected some additional photos there. His next stop was a camera shop where he rented a movie camera and a projector. And finally, Dave went to FAO Schwarz and purchased a toy drum.

Over the next week, the package of photos from The Bahamas came in and he worked on the presentation. He photographed all the elements, including some graphics he created, filmed the assembly with the movie camera, and then brought the 8 mm film to a lab for processing.

When the brief reel was completed, Dave reviewed it and was delighted with the outcome. *It won't get me the job, but it will dazzle Elisa. And it will be a great addition to my portfolio.*

On the day of the presentation, Elisa and Tiffany both sat in the conference room. Dave showed up with a large cardboard box which aroused their curiosity. He took out the projector and plugged it in. Since there was no projection screen in the room, he focused it on an empty wall. When he removed the drum from the box, they looked at each other and began to laugh. Tiffany said, "Did you buy yourself a new toy?" And they laughed some more.

As the 30-second film began to play on the wall, Dave started tapping on the drum in a rapid staccato beat, rata-tata-tata-tata through the entire film, playing even louder and faster at the end. The film was a series of dazzling photos of Caribbean scenes, flashing on-screen so fast you could hardly see the images. The drumbeat created excitement, and the mesmerizing technique made you want to see more detail in each photo. At the end, the logo of the island appeared on the screen for a few seconds before fading to black.

The two women were stunned. Neither could speak as Dave waited for a compliment of some kind. Finally, Elisa said, "Could you play it again?"

After rewinding the film, Dave played it again, including his drum solo.

When they didn't comment, Dave said, "Look this is just a comp. I didn't know how to show you the concept with a storyboard, so I created it in film with stock photography. Don't you like it?"

Elisa jumped up, saying, "I get it. Wait right here." And she ran out of the office.

She was back in five minutes with two men. They stood in the tiny room and without introduction, she said, "Play it one more time."

Dave ran it again with as much energy as he could put into the drumbeat. And he waited.

One of the men finally blurted out, "Holy shit! That's amazing!" Turning to Dave, he said, "Hi, I'm Jerry Wantah. Robbie was right when he told me about your talent. Welcome to DBB."

Later, Elisa sat in her office, crushed by the outcome of the meeting. When she had seen Dave's concept, she immediately recognized it was brilliant. She had known she couldn't send him away without showing it to Wantah. Certain he would like it, she planned to produce it herself. *I never expected Mr. Wantah would hire Dave on the spot. I am so screwed. He will take my job and destroy my career at this agency.*

CHAPTER 37

Unexpected Outcome

DAVE'S GOALS had been to show Elisa that she was wrong when she prejudged him and also to create a TV commercial concept that he could use to get a job in the ad business. He never expected to be offered a job at DBB. It was the hottest ad agency in New York City, turning the industry upside down with its creativity. But here he was.

Dave was responsible for the entire tourism campaign, including TV, magazine ads, and travel agency posters. The best part was the opportunity to direct the photography for the ads on location in the Caribbean, and maybe take some of his own photos to be used in the advertising.

※ ※ ※

Elisa's expectations had also been way off the mark. Initially, she was certain that Dave would fail at the assignment. His submission would be rejected as being unprofessional. And that would have been the end of his quest for a job at DBB. However, she underestimated him and the ad concept turned out great.

When she saw his presentation, her plan was to complete it herself. She was even prepared to pay him a bonus for his effort and possibly use him for some of the photography.

She never expected Wantah to jump over her and directly offer him a job. Now she was stuck with this country hick. And he was going to be huge trouble for her going forward, even with his good ideas.

As Group Creative Director, Elisa was one of the few females in that role at any of the top ad agencies. She now had three art directors working for her, including Dave. And her group handled a pool of highly prestigious clients.

The campaign was a smashing success, winning industry accolades and countless awards, plus generating a huge flow of tourism traffic for the client. As a result, the agency got additional recognition, Elisa's star rose higher, and Dave was the hottest new find on Madison Avenue. He also jumped over the other art directors to become the lead creative in her group.

While the entire episode worked in Elisa's favor, she was still upset that Dave proved her wrong. And it did nothing to diminish the tension that remained in their relationship. It also further boosted his self-confidence, which increased her fear of him and the strain between them. *He's going to take my job just with his attitude.*

CHAPTER 38

The Boundaries Remain

Elisa's creative group had one win after another, experiencing unprecedented success. After getting word that they had won several additional awards, Dave suggested they meet for drinks after work and celebrate their accomplishments.

Tiffany recommended P.J. Clarke's on Third Avenue, and the entire department went there. Clarke's had been a popular landmark at that location since 1884. The bar and most of the fixtures looked like they had been there since the saloon opened and, as usual, the place was packed with a boisterous after-work crowd.

Dave bought the first round and toasted Elisa for putting together this creative team. After a couple of drinks, they moved to a large table in the back and ordered some appetizers.

By 9 p.m., despite everyone having had too much to drink, no one made a move to leave. Tiffany started to hit on Dave, who ignored her attempts. Elisa, seeing this, was not pleased. As ten o'clock approached, the other two art directors took their leave, along with most of the remaining staff.

Tiffany stayed, hoping to hook up with Dave. However, Elisa was not having it. She took her by the arm and said, "C'mon, I'm putting you in a cab."

Dave paid the remaining tab and followed them out. After Elisa got Tiffany in a taxi, she turned to Dave and told him she was going to walk home. When asked where she lived, she told him it was only about five blocks south and over on Second Avenue.

He walked her to her apartment building, and when she didn't invite him up, he gave her a brief hug and thanked her for the opportunity to work together. She was pleased by his gesture and was thankful he didn't push to come up to her place. The tension that started when he interviewed for the job remained with her.

Dave was living in a residence hotel on the Westside and decided to walk home rather than take a cab. He wanted to clear his head and shake off the effects of the alcohol.

Walking across town, Dave thought about the evening and was embarrassed by Tiffany's brazen moves on him. *She's not someone I want to get entangled with. She is immature and obviously looking for a husband, but it won't be me.*

Reflecting further, Dave realized he hadn't made much progress on improving his relationship with Elisa. While finding her attractive, he couldn't get past the protective wall she erected. His feeling was that she used this cold and private façade as a defense mechanism. *It's almost certainly driven by her insecurity. I'm convinced there is a warm person behind that bluster.*

Thinking about Elisa brought back thoughts of losing his mother at such an early age. He missed her nurturing and warmth, having never given that affection a second thought. He only saw the discipline. He smiled remembering what she had taught him about affection, love, and sexual interaction, and how it had impacted his comfort level with women. *I wish I could discuss it with her now. I still know very little about it.*

CHAPTER 39

Not Her Type

THE GROUP CONTINUED to develop outstanding advertising that was getting praise from the industry, including a brief article in *Advertising Age*. It featured Elisa as one of the few women in the creative director position in the city, comparing her to the well-known ad agency star Mary Wells.

When Dave read the article, his first thought was the notoriety would further insulate Elisa from her staff.

A few of Dave's new clients required a large number of newspaper and magazine print ads. Although he liked TV better, these ads brought him back to his roots. One client was a clothing retailer that was planning to open stores in major cities across the country.

Dave designed a format for the ad campaign and ran it by Elisa. She commented, "The type is all wrong. Why are you using Bookman Bold for the headlines?"

"I selected it because it has weight. It's bold and strong. It's readable and speaks to a male audience."

Giving him a stern look with her eyes drilling into him, she replied, "But it's very ordinary. Use Baskerville Bold. It accomplishes your need for strength, and it adds style. After all, we're selling fashion here, even if it's men's fashion."

"Elisa, you're overthinking it. No one will notice the difference."

"I will notice the difference. I worked in a type shop and set type by hand. It's where I began my career. If there's anything I know in this business, it's type fonts."

"I still don't think it's that important."

"Listen to me. Selection and layout of type are critical to the look of the ad. Look past the photography. You must always be intensely selective with type. It's often the difference between an average ad and a great one."

Walking back to his office, Dave realized she was right, and he wasn't paying enough attention to the type fonts he was selecting. But he thought she could have delivered the message in a more congenial way. When she finished her critique, he felt like an army private, and thought he had to salute her as his sergeant.

In a way, he felt sorry for her. She was constantly under enormous pressure from the management team, the account executives, and from the clients themselves. Just last week she was crucified for a typo on the address in an ad prepared by one of the mechanical artists. No one caught the error, not the client nor the account exec. But she took the blame and got hammered. It was all about being a woman in this male-dominated industry.

His job was the most fun he could imagine. Hers should be, as well. But it was constant pressure. *I want to find a way to make it easier for her. And I want to hug her, but it would be like caressing a giant block of ice.*

CHAPTER 40

Freelance Opportunity

Rᴏʙʙɪᴇ ᴍᴇᴛ ᴅᴀᴠᴇ for lunch following a meeting he had with Jerry Wantah. They went to Mike Manuche's, had a couple of drinks, and ordered lunch. Robbie asked Dave how the job was going.

"It's a great job at an exciting time in New York. Creativity is king in advertising right now, and every agency is trying to outdo each other. I'm loving the work."

"How are you getting along with Elisa?"

"I know what she's going through, so I overlook her attitude. But she's not easy."

"The guys upstairs don't like her. She may not last long."

"She puts up with a lot of shit from them. Last week, one of the flunky assistant AEs yelled at her over a typo, and then he asked her out. And he's married."

'Well, you'd better get used to it. Everybody is screwing anything in a skirt. The women want to get laid as much as the men do. These horny broads are all over me when we get together for drinks."

"I'm not sure you're right. I think they're looking for husbands and using sex to get there."

"Dave, don't be naive. Some of them are more sex-starved than us."

"Maybe you're right. I'm not out there that much and I'm still not comfortable with the dating scene. I haven't dated since I moved to the city, and I certainly didn't date in Indian Lake."

"In that case, we're going out one night and get you laid. It's so easy these days. All you've got to do is show up."

"All right. Let's get together one night soon."

"Okay, so much for the broads. I have an opportunity for you. I have a small client that needs some freelance work, and I told him about you. We're meeting him for drinks tomorrow night. He's starting a small fishing magazine, and it has lots of potential."

"That sounds great. I'd love to work with anyone who deals with the outdoors."

Jimmy Jones was bigger than life. He was a huge man with an even larger personality and a ruddy face. Robbie knew him from the Adirondacks, where he grew up. Jimmy's father had owned a large tract of land at the edge of the town of Lake George. As the town grew, so did the value of the property. The land was sold after a bidding war for it, and Jones inherited the money a couple of years ago.

Pushing back his wildly tousled dark red hair, Jones explained to Dave his vision was to produce a magazine that promoted freshwater fishing as an exciting sport. The challenge was the perception of fishing as a slow, boring waste of time.

Dave immediately conjured up images of whitewater rapids with a fisherman in waders fighting a large brown trout. He described that scene to Jones and added, "Yes, I can deliver on that brand concept. And I can create an ad campaign to generate a lot of interest for the magazine. Having lived in the Adirondacks, I appreciate your vision."

Putting out his huge, calloused hand, Jones said, "You get it. Let's move forward!"

CHAPTER 41

Flexing Egos

ROBBIE CALLED DAVE the following week and told him how excited Jones was about working with him. "Your ideas resonated with his vision. I was impressed by how quickly you came up with that concept. With your creative mind, I can get you lots of freelance business."

Dave was pleased with the feedback and the possibility of additional clients. While he loved doing the TV commercials for the agency's major accounts, he didn't like the baggage that came with the clients and the account executives. His heart was more into helping small companies compete with their huge competitors and become successful. It all went back to his entrepreneurial experience with the fireworks caper and the small firms in the Adirondacks.

An assistant account executive on one of the agency's largest accounts was in Elisa's office. His name was Rodney Klein, and he was complaining about a missed deadline on an ad. This client had a reputation for always demanding impossible delivery dates that were often arbitrary.

Tall and thin with unruly hair, Klein wore glasses with Coke-bottle lenses and his clothes always gave the impression that he'd just slept in them. He was shouting so loud Dave could hear him in his office. Offended by his foul language, Dave walked down to Elisa's office and got in his face. "If you can't control your mouth, then get out of here. . . now."

"Who the fuck are you to tell me how to talk? Get back in the hole you crawled out of and mind your own business."

"When you abuse my boss, it is my business. I warned you. Don't say another word. Just leave. Now."

As the AE started to respond, Dave grabbed his arm and pulled him out of Elisa's office. Frightened, she said, "Dave, don't. Please."

Ignoring her, Dave said, "Get on the elevator, and don't come back here until you apologize to her."

"I don't apologize to women."

"In that case, don't ever come back down here."

Pointing a finger at Dave, he said, "You're Powers, right? You don't know who you're fucking with. You'll be out of here by the end of the week." And he turned and walked onto the elevator.

Dave went back into Elisa's office and closed the door. He hadn't noticed, but she was crying. Wiping her tears, she said, "You should never have done that. You're in serious trouble now."

"That little shit can't hurt me. He's a jerk and needs to grow up."

"He can hurt you. The account supervisor is his uncle and he protects him. He will get you fired."

"Elisa, you don't know me very well. I've survived far bigger challenges than this little piece of shit and his bureaucratic uncle. Let me take you to dinner tonight. You need a break."

"I would like to, but I can't. You don't know how toxic you are right now. I can't be seen with you. Please go back to your office."

Walking back, Dave was flabbergasted. He couldn't understand how this insignificant twit, who contributed nothing to the success of the company, could have him fired. And Elisa, at her management level, had to take crap from him.

Dave was also troubled by how frightened Elisa was of this

insolent brat. *She didn't thank me for interceding, or even acknowledge it.* He knew now he had a crush on her, but it was hopeless. *If she gave me the chance to get close, I could break her out of this stranglehold. But she will never let it happen.*

Rather than resume work, he returned to his office, grabbed his jacket, and left the building for the day.

CHAPTER 42

Girl Interrupted

FRUSTRATED AND ANGRY, Dave needed a change of scenery. He called Robbie and said, "Hey buddy, I need a diversion. It's been a day from hell. Let's do the bars tonight."

"Meet me at Clarke's at six-thirty. That place is always jumping and a great place to start."

Dave got there first and stood at the bar. He ordered a beer and waited for Robbie. Sitting at a stool next to him was a tall, full-figured woman with red hair and dark eyes. When he looked over, she gave him a big, pleasant smile. Responding to her, he said, "Are you here alone?"

With a strong accent, she said, "Aye, mate, I am. Stella's me nyme."

"Hi, Stella. You sound like you're from England."

"Right on. I'm 'ere visiting with me mum and dad, touring the city. They're really a delight, but I needed some time by m'self. They went off to the theater t'night, but I begged off. I saw a chance to get out on me own." Touching his arm, she asked, "So, what's your story?"

"I work in the city. In advertising. And what do you do?"

"How exciting. I work for a solicitor in London. 'Ave ya been across the pond?"

"No. I've lived here and upstate New York, but I haven't traveled much beyond that."

Stella turned to face him full on and leaned forward provocatively. Her low-cut top revealed two very large breasts with enormous cleavage. Dave drank in the view and thought, *I'd need a ladder to get to the bottom of that.* The lecherous look was not lost on Stella.

Now, running her hand down his arm, she said, "Yu're a 'andsome man. Do ya find me attractive?"

"Yes, you're very attractive."

"Would ya like to 'ave sex with me?"

Catching his breath, he answered, "I would love to have sex with you."

"Then what the bloody 'ell are we doin 'ere?"

As they raced out the door, Robbie walked in. Dave turned and said, "Hi Robbie. I have to leave to take care of something, but I'll see you later."

Seeing the woman who was with him, Robbie grinned. "Well, have fun."

Stella took Dave to the hotel room that she shared with her parents, explaining that they wouldn't return until much later after the play had ended. Once inside, she began to strip down, so Dave did the same.

Turning toward Stella as she removed her bra, he was taken by how large her breasts were. Not only were they massive, but they were almost too big, particularly her nipples and areolas which he found unattractive. However, they were beautifully shaped and mesmerizing.

With a pile of clothes on each side of the bed, they jumped in and began fondling each other. About one minute later, her parents walked into the room. Her mother shouted, "Stella, what on earth?" Her father came at Dave wielding the cane he used to walk.

Scooping up his clothes, Dave dodged the swinging cane and rushed to the door saying, "It's okay. I was just using the toilet."

Once in the hall which, fortunately, was empty, he put on his clothes and ran for his life. He couldn't wait to get back to Clarke's to share his adventure with Robbie.

CHAPTER 43

Exodus Strategy

On MONDAY MORNING, Dave found a note on his desk to immediately report to the Human Resources Vice President, Maxwell Dealman. By the time he got upstairs, he was furious. But he held his tongue.

Sitting at a small conference table in a large, well-appointed office, the VP and his assistant awaited his arrival. He motioned to a chair on the opposite side of the table and said, "Mr. Powers, we've had a complaint that you raised your voice and manhandled one of the other employees. That is a serious offense." As he said it in his starchy manner, his assistant sat there solemnly nodding.

Angry at the accusation, Dave answered, "Did he tell you that he verbally abused my manager, using expletives? And he did the same to me."

"No one filed a complaint of that nature about him. And frankly, at this point, it sounds like retribution."

"Should I file a formal complaint?"

"I would strongly advise against it. And since this is your first transgression, I'm going to give you a written warning, and put you on probation for three months." Handing him the document, he continued, "If you have no further questions, you may leave now. And I expect more mature behavior from you in the future."

"And I expect the same from the immature brat that filed the complaint. If he disrespects any of us again, I will file a complaint. Be sure to let him know that. And let his uncle know, as well."

Dave stood and walked out without saying another word. Instead of going down to his office, he left the building and went to a coffee shop to calm down. *The bureaucratic machine is working efficiently, crushing anyone who doesn't conform. I have to leave this agency, but I'll do it on my schedule when I'm ready, not when Blowhard tells me.*

Returning to his office, he stopped by to report his meeting to Elisa. She had already received a copy of his written warning, so she was aware of what occurred. She said, "Dave, you were lucky. You won't be the next time."

"Don't worry, there won't be a next time. I don't know how long I can put up with this uneven playing field."

Having difficulty looking at him, she said, "Yes, management came down on you unfairly. But remember, you originally got the job the same way."

"Are you sorry for the way I secured my position here?"

Now smiling, she answered, "No. You proved you were more than up to the task. Now get to work."

Back in his office, Dave called Robbie and arranged for them to meet for lunch. Robbie told him to be at the Supreme Macaroni Company on 9th Avenue at noon.

Dave arrived at the address and assessed the dingy storefront. He thought he was walking into a drug den disguised as a grocery store, but it was a pasta wholesale/retail business. It also contained a small casual restaurant in the back. The entire place was covered in a fine layer of flour dust. Robbie ordered two "Special Cokes" and two orders of pappardelle with Bolognese sauce. The waiter brought out two glasses of wine in recycled Coca Cola bottles. Only in New York.

Dave asked, "What happened to you Friday night? I was back there in less than a half-hour and you were gone."

"Then I guess you didn't get laid."

"We won't go there right now, but let me tell you what's happening at work."

Sharing the office confrontation and resulting probation with Robbie, Dave added, "I'm going to leave when the time is right and start my own agency. And I wanted to ask you if you have any prospects other than Jimmy Jones?"

"Yes, I have a couple of others, but they are not quite ready to launch. You should also know that Jones is planning on publishing an entire series of outdoor magazines."

"Yes, he told me, and I'm excited about that. But I can't start a business with one client, regardless of their size."

"Then hang on for another month or two. I think I'll have some other business for you by then."

"How about if we set up a commission arrangement on any clients you bring in?"

"I would love that. I would devote more time to getting you business. Can you afford to pay commissions as you start up?"

"I have some money from my dad's estate, so I can pay as we go. I just don't want to launch a business until I can cover the overhead."

"Smart thinking. I'll start pushing some advertising. How about another *Coke* before we go?"

Leaving The Mothership

CHAPTER 44

The Warning

THE EXCITEMENT grew as Dave began to plan his new venture. He filed a certificate for a new business which he called Image Concepts. He liked the name because it left no doubt about the company's focus.

Finding an affordable loft for the operation was more difficult. He wanted to be in midtown near where his clients would be located, but the rent rates for office space there were off the charts. He finally rented space in an old, converted warehouse on East 48th Street. He took 1,000 square feet of the top floor, with another 3,000 feet available if he later decided to expand. Until he had a book of business, though, he had no plans to hire anyone.

After opening an account at a local bank, he ordered a phone line and was then able to design and print stationery, as well as business cards for Robbie and himself.

He continued to work at DBB until he had a few more accounts, but he was counting the days. After reviewing a storyboard with Elisa, he again asked her out to dinner. In a firm voice, she said, "Dave, I don't want to date you. We work together and we've got to limit it to that."

"What if I weren't working here?"

She replied softly, "Look, I'm just not interested in dating anyone right now. Please don't be offended."

✻ ✻ ✻

That afternoon, Elisa had another run-in with the same assistant AE, Rodney Klein. This time he was demanding an impossible delivery of a new ad campaign. When he began to raise his voice, she put her hand up, walked to the door, and called Tiffany into her office. Tiffany came in and sat down in the chair next to Klein. She wrinkled her nose as she caught the body odor coming off him. Leaning away, she thought, *What a disgusting individual. He probably hasn't showered in a week. Or combed his hair, for that matter.*

Pointing to the pad in Tiffany's hand, Elisa then said to him, "Now, tell me again when you want this campaign ready."

He politely said, "I want it in one week, without fail. And then he got up to leave and said, "Be careful. You're walking on eggs, and you're going to ruin more than your expensive shoes."

Dave had been on the phone in his office when he heard Klein's loud voice coming through the wall. When he hung up, he walked to Elisa's office just as Tiffany went in and sat next to Klein in the only other chair in the room. Dave began pacing back and forth to let him know he was there. Klein kept looking up at Dave's stare drilling into him.

When Klein entered the hallway, Dave got in his face with an exaggerated smile and said, "Hello, Kleen. Nice to see you slumming in our neighborhood. I hope you're having a Kleen-language day. Oh, and take the elevator, not the stairs. I'd hate to see you fall down the stairs and blemish your handsome face."

Now in a rage from the disrespect he was getting from Elisa's staff, he snarled, "Powers, you are so fucked. I'm getting you fired!"

"Brilliant choice of words, *Kleen*. We only allow *Kleen* language on this floor. You don't want me to file a complaint, do you? Now go back to your cave. It's starting to smell around here."

Elisa saw the confrontation but chose to ignore it. She turned to Tiffany and said, "Anytime you see Klein walk into my office, you come right in and sit down. It may be the only way I can stop his abusive language."

"Yes, but how do you keep from vomiting? He smells like a garbage truck."

When Elisa was alone again, she breathed deeply. *Despite this stopgap measure, my days are numbered here.*

CHAPTER 45

The Departure

BEFORE DAVE had a chance to buy furniture for the new space, Robbie came through with two new clients. The first was a small menswear manufacturer that was introducing a line of men's fragrances. After English Leather and Canoe hit the market, this became a hot new category, and Dave was thrilled to get the client.

The second client was a large photo processing company. They wanted to capitalize on the popular snapshot market and were launching a line of inexpensive cameras to compete with Kodak.

Dave went to Elisa and told her he was leaving to start his own agency. Expecting he would be quitting at some point, she said, "After that probation incident, I knew you'd leave. But I was sure you'd go to another agency. I never expected you to start your own shop."

"When I was a kid living not far from your place, I launched a little money-making gig and caught the entrepreneur bug. This will be my third full-time business, and I'm excited about the clients I'm starting out with."

"Dave, you're very talented and there's no doubt you'll succeed. My only advice is to have patience with your clients. They are all demanding and expect miracles every day."

"Thank you, Elisa. When do you want me to leave?"

"Why don't you finish up the print campaign you're on and wrap up production on the new TV commercial."

"I can have both done in a week and if you need me longer, I'll stay on."

"Finish those assignments and you can go. I'm sure you're anxious to get started on your new venture. Knowing you, it will be exciting."

On his last day, the department took him out for drinks after work. They went to a small bar near the office and celebrated his new agency. They all asked questions about the new shop, and Dave mentioned the new accounts as he gave out business cards to each of them. They were all impressed with the strength of his client base.

Before long, Tiffany was again hitting on him, and like the first time, he became embarrassed. He could also see the annoyance in Elisa's eyes, but she let it go. Dave was uncomfortable and couldn't wait to leave. After his second drink, he shook hands with the guys, kissed the women, and left.

Despite the distance, he walked back to his dreary hotel room promising himself that if he held the new accounts, he would find an attractive apartment. He was exhilarated about getting started Monday morning and couldn't wait to get there.

When Elisa got home, she made a cup of chamomile tea and thought about her department without Dave. *I was scared to death of him the first time I met him, and yet I can't imagine what it's going to be like without him. But he still scares me. He's so damn cocky.*

CHAPTER 46

Starting Over, Again

Dave ARRIVED at his new office bright and early Monday morning, excited to get going. He began work on the two new clients, preparing ad designs for both of them. He worked through lunch and completed both concepts in the early afternoon.

Robbie called him at four o'clock and told him he had set up an appointment with a financial advisory firm on Wall Street for Thursday morning. Robbie's description of Dave's work got them interested in meeting with Dave, as they wanted something different. The CEO was looking to get away from the stodgy bank-style financial advertising and wanted to communicate excitement and energy.

The advisory company's luxurious conference room had views of downtown New York and parts of Brooklyn from the 30th floor. From the reception desk to the CEO's office, the entire place exuded financial success and luxury. When they walked into the meeting, the CEO was flanked by two of his executives. Instead of three-piece suits, they wore open-collar shirts and casual slacks. Dave knew immediately he would sell them.

Robbie handed each of them a folder containing ads for the Caribbean account, as Dave set up the projector and ran the TV commercial. That's all it took. The CEO said, "Dave, if you can deliver that kind of enthusiasm for us, you have the account."

"Sir, we don't sell products and services. We fulfill dreams. Here's how we'll work. Whoever will be our agency coordinator needs to provide a data package with everything you can tell us about your company. We'll send you a proposal with our fees, and we will present a concept campaign in two weeks. If it's acceptable, then we have a deal."

※ ※ ※

The following week, Dave got a phone call. "Is this Dave Powers? This is Steve Dudar. You probably don't remember me, but when you came to work at DBB, I was an expediter in the Account Services Department. You always treated me the same way you treated the account supervisors and executives."

"I'm sorry, I don't remember you. There were so many guys in Account Services, but I treat everyone the same. It's who I am."

"And that's why I'm calling you. I was working there to learn the ad business. My family owns a specialty manufacturing firm that makes high-end office furniture and lighting for offices and showrooms."

"Are you still at the agency?"

"No, I'm back at our company and I'll be handling the marketing. I'd like you to come in and see if you'd be interested in handling our advertising account."

"Absolutely. I'd be delighted to meet with you. Again, I apologize for not remembering you."

After the call, Dave realized that if these two new accounts were added to his client list, he would have to hire staff right away. Jimmy Jones had already told him to start work on the next two magazines he was launching.

He called Richard Guerrero at Bahamas Bank and told him he had launched a new venture and already had a couple of additional accounts. He had previously forwarded his business plan, which Guerrero had blessed.

"Congratulations, Dave. I'm delighted, but not surprised to hear how quickly you've set up your company. Please be cautious and pay attention to the business. New York is a cruel town that finds weaknesses and attacks them. I assume you need some working capital."

"Yes, I'd like to draw fifty thousand."

"That sounds about right. Give me the bank information and I'll transfer it."

After the call, Dave started to think about staffing. He needed an assistant to keep him organized and do the books, and he had to hire one or two art directors. He didn't know where to start.

CHAPTER 47

The Scapegoat

Elisa sat in her office, struggling to juggle her department's workload. It was becoming apparent how important Dave had been in getting projects completed on schedule. With him gone, the other two art directors started slacking off. They both were certain management preferred a man in the position, and they each knew if they got her out, one of them would probably replace her.

The creative services VP, Dealman, sent her a note to attend a meeting the following morning. She walked into the conference room to find him sitting at the large table flanked by all his assistant AEs, including Klein. He pointed to a single chair on the opposite side of the table. Dealman presented her with a list of shortcomings that needed immediate remedy. They included deteriorating relations with the account service staff, a noticeable difference in the quality of the creative product, and a much higher percentage of missed delivery dates. Klein, who sat on the VPs right, gloated at her discomfort.

Appalled by the criticism, she countered that the charges were overblown. Elisa also pointed out that Dave's departure without a replacement was affecting both scheduling and quality. Plus, they hadn't approved her requisition to hire a new art director.

He responded, "Remember, you didn't want to hire him in the first place. Now you're using his absence as an excuse?"

Elisa became enraged, knowing they were aware of the huge

increase in volume of orders. She defended all the charges on his list to no avail. He ended the conversation by saying he expected a substantial improvement over the next 60 days.

She walked back to her office knowing she was being set up to fail as a result of activity she had no control over. *It's time. I have to find a new job.*

A major advertising awards ceremony was coming up, and Elisa decided to attend it and see if any job opportunities were floating around. She got to the cocktail party early and networked the crowd, meeting up with acquaintances and striking up chatter with strangers.

When she sat down at her table for dinner, there was a conversation going on about women in the advertising business. Most of the talk was about Mary Wells, the female superstar in the New York market. One of the other ladies at the table brought up the fact that it was so difficult for females to excel in the field, regardless of talent.

Elisa made a wine-induced comment that despite the success of her campaigns, and her position as a group creative director, she was being held back in this male-dominated industry.

Unfortunately, there was a man at the table who took note of her comment. He knew who she was, but she was not aware he worked for one of the advertising publications. In his column the following week, he quoted her comment without mentioning her name.

The day after his column was published, he got several calls to identify the woman mentioned in the story. One of the callers who knew the reporter personally was an executive at DBB, and the columnist confidentially revealed the name to him.

Two months after her disastrous meeting with the VP, Dealman again called her to a meeting in his conference room. Flanked by his team, he announced his conclusion that there was no improvement in his list of complaints. "In fact," he said, "The situation is worsening. I'm moving you from your creative director position and returning you to an art director role."

In an out-of-character response, she exploded. "You bastard!

That's not going to happen. You deliberately put me in this position so you can demote me. I guess I was too strong or didn't have enough testosterone for you *men* in the executive suite. Or maybe it was because I didn't put out. I'm done. I'll have my office cleaned out by the end of the day."

Klein laughed at her tirade, embarrassing his uncle, the VP.

As she got up to leave, she leaned across the table and got in Klein's face. "Nice play, you dumb jerk. If it weren't for your uncle here, your smelly ass would be riding the back of a sanitation truck, dumping trash cans."

Then it was the other AEs' turn to laugh. As Elisa walked out of the meeting, she turned to the VP and said, "You need to do a better job of teaching your *boys* some manners and keeping them in line, or *you'll* be looking for a new job."

Elisa stood tall and walked out. *Boy, did that feel good!*

CHAPTER 48

The Job Search

With an updated portfolio and resumé, Elisa hit the phones, trying to make appointments for an interview. First she called on people she knew in the industry and then went through the list of major ad agencies. Finally, she contacted the mid-size shops. After an entire week of phone calls and in-person visits to ad agency HR departments, she did not get one interview.

Something was not right. Her portfolio was one of the best in the city, much too strong not to get a meeting with even one of the mid-size agencies. Elisa called a close friend at another agency and asked him to investigate the situation. There had to be a reason she couldn't get any appointments.

He called back the next day and told her that she had been blackballed. Word had gotten out about her comments at DBB, and no one would touch her. There was a buzz around the agencies that she wasn't performing up to expectation and was bitter about her deserved demotion. No one wants to hire someone with baggage, especially a woman.

When Dave heard she left DBB, he called the agency and asked Tiffany what happened. She told him Elisa pissed off the creative VP and he was getting his revenge. It was going to be very difficult for her to get a decent job anywhere in the city. He then asked her for Elisa's phone number. Before hanging up, Tiffany suggested, "Let's meet for a drink one evening." He told her they would sometime, but he was too busy with his fledgling agency right now.

Dave immediately called Elisa and left her a message to call back. When she didn't return his call, he tried again and left another message. His third message said, "I'm picking you up at your apartment tomorrow night at seven and taking you to dinner. Refusal is not an acceptable option. I may take the door down if you don't open it."

Sitting at his drafting table, Dave looked around at the bare brick walls and wire-glass industrial windows and thought, *How am I going to get her to work in this shithole after she was an executive at the plush offices of DBB?*

He had been so busy from day one, he had never gotten around to setting up a proper office structure. Even the elevator looked like a small version of the freight elevator. He knew he needed her touch to make it a desirable place to work, rather than a warehouse loft.

CHAPTER 49

The Proposition

S ITTING IN MAXWELL'S PLUM with a bottle of Soave Bolla, Dave looked at Elisa and saw that she was still uncomfortable in his presence. While he wolfed down a T-bone steak, she picked at her veal piccata and barely ate her salad.

He gave her time to relax in his presence before saying, "Okay, now tell me what happened."

"For once, I'm going to be brutally honest with you and go back to the beginning. When you first came to my office, I was upset that you came in through the executive suite. Strike One. You were a hillbilly from the mountains, except you didn't bring your banjo. And you had a portfolio to match. Strike Two. And you had all this self-confidence leaking out of your eyes. For me, that was Strike Three."

"What does self-confidence have to do with it?"

Exhaling, she said, "As a woman in this field, you can never relax. You've got to be better than the men, and you still come in second. You were so cock-sure of yourself, even with that shit portfolio. It scared the hell out of me. I was certain you could take my job just with your attitude."

"Boy, is that a reach."

"Not at the time. But you proved to be someone special, and you actually improved my stature in the company. Your creativity reflected on me. We were almost always on time. You defended me against the macho males upstairs. Then when you left, it all crashed down around me."

Sarcastically, Dave said, "So, I'm responsible for you losing your job."

"No, no. They wanted me out because I wasn't one of the boys. But I was easily as good as the other group creative directors, all of them male."

"You were certainly better, but why can't you get a job anywhere? Did you kick your boss in the nuts on your way out?"

With a little pride in her voice, she answered, "In a manner of speaking, yes. I did it verbally, but it was more of a stomp than a kick. I told him why he was pushing me out, and he didn't like hearing it. And then I crushed his nephew's microscopic wiener in front of the arrogant creep and the other AEs. Boy, did that feel good."

Dave refilled their glasses. "Now it's my turn to be brutally honest. I'm glad you got pushed out and I'm delighted you can't find a job."

"You bastard! Did I treat you that bad?"

"Sort of, but I was convinced it was a defense mechanism. I kept trying to see past your protective façade. I was sure you didn't dislike me, but you wouldn't let me get close. Tonight, I got you to come to dinner kicking and screaming. It took three calls and a threat on your life."

"I'm glad you called. I'm just embarrassed, that's all. But why are you pleased I can't get a job?"

The crème brûlée came, so Dave decided to let her stew a little longer while they had some dessert.

Elisa tasted a bite of the creamy confection. "Are you ever going to answer my question?"

"Yes." Savoring a spoonful of his, he waited until he swallowed it. "It's because now I'm going to proposition you."

She stiffened, but he smiled. "Actually, I have a proposition for you. I'm not going to offer you a job. I'm presenting you with an opportunity. Come to work for me. I will pay you whatever DBB was paying you, and if you can stand sharing an office with me for six months, I'll make you a partner."

Frowning, she replied, "A partner in an agency with no accounts?"

With a big smirk, Dave said, "You are one tough-ass broad. You've been working with the wrong men too long. My little agency has three regional clients and five national clients, soon to be ten or twelve. I already have more work than both of us can handle, and more than your department produced, but now we have the media and production billing in addition to the creative fees. So, does my offer sound a little better to you?"

"Wow! Where did you get all that business?"

Adding sarcasm to his smirk, he answered, "From the toothless and barefoot mountain hicks in those little towns in the Adirondacks, where else? I even got a banjo account."

That got her, and she started laughing. "No, really. How did you land that much business so fast?"

"My friend who introduced me to DBB has lots of contacts at big companies. He's working for me on commission. So, did you decide yet? The offer is perishable. It comes off the table with the dirty dishes."

"Well, I do need a job."

"A job? This isn't a job I'm offering. Finish your crème brûlée before I eat it."

They finished their dessert in silence and kept looking up at each other and smiling. Dave offered her coffee, but she turned it down. He paid the check and they left.

They took a cab back to her place, and he said, "Before you get excited, I'm not coming up."

Elisa answered with a big smile and a sideways glance. "I didn't invite you."

"Here's my card. Be at the office by nine tomorrow. We have a lot of work to do."

She kissed him on the cheek and got out. He watched her enter the building and gave his address to the driver to take him home. When he got in his room, he swung his fist in the air and shouted, "Yes!"

CHAPTER 50

Organizational Skills

ALTHOUGH DAVE had taken all the basic steps to establish a business, he did nothing to properly set up the physical office. People entering the nondescript industrial building were welcomed by a passenger elevator with a filthy cabin. The office was an open area in the corner of a large unfinished loft with no interior walls. The exterior walls were brick, the floor concrete with 50-year-old stains, and the floor-to-ceiling windows were made of small wire-glass panes.

When Elisa got off the elevator at 8:45 a.m., she wasn't surprised by the appearance of the office. She liked the furniture Dave had bought, but he'd left it scattered around near the elevator. She shook her head. *Wow, there's a lot of work to be done here.*

Dave jumped up from his drafting table and said, "Good morning, and welcome to my prison. You'll be housed in jail cell two, as soon as I build it."

Elisa laughed. "You really did rent a detention facility, but you gave it a woman's touch."

Laughing, he offered her coffee and pound cake from a small table. "Let's sit down in my office and talk."

"Your office? I don't see any offices here. Is the landlord going to build out the space? What's the plan?"

"The deal I made with the owner is a lease for the net space of

1,000 square feet at ghetto rent rates. I can improve it however I want, and I can take more of the floor as we need it. I agree it's a mess right now, but it does have character."

"That's not the word I'd use to describe it, but let's work on a floor plan right away. We can't have clients visiting us with the place looking like this."

They spent the next couple of hours designing the offices, measuring off the space, and marking the floor with tape. They both liked the idea of an open-space office, so they designed a few private offices along the wall, plus a large conference room and a bullpen for the creative team.

The building owner had given Dave the name of a construction company that specialized in interior office buildouts. As soon as he and Elisa completed the floor plan, he called them. Dave also got permission from the owner to have the elevator cabin upgraded at his own expense.

After the phone calls, it was lunchtime. They went down to a neighborhood pizza parlor and, over slices of pepperoni pizza, discussed the workload. Dave told her that there was a backlog of projects that they had to get into production right away. They both spent the next two weeks working long hours getting all the ads completed and placed in the publications.

Robbie stopped over one day to see the offices. He also had some news to share. When he walked off the elevator, his reaction was similar to Elisa's. Used to luxury living, he remarked, "What a shithole."

Dave laughed and said, "Congratulations on your architectural taste. The construction starts next week. In another month you won't recognize this place. I'm even having the wire-glass windows and the skylight redone. The elevator will also be upgraded to look like new."

Elisa came over and Dave introduced her. Robbie shook her hand and couldn't take his eyes off her. "You used to work at DBB, didn't you? We never met, but I knew about you. I'm glad you're here." Pointing to Dave, he added, "Keep this guy grounded. He's a dreamer."

"Yes, I'm already experiencing that and it's frightening."

Turning to Dave, he said, "I'll have a new client ready to meet in the next couple of weeks. I also left my family's printing business and went to work for another printer where I'll be on full commission. Between that and the money I'll make here, I can keep my wife in luxury without her using her own money."

"I'm delighted you have a new client coming on board, but is leaving the family business a smart move? It will be your company someday."

"The commission arrangement puts big money in my pocket now, and that's important. The family operation would pay off way down the road. Although my older brother has Hodgkin's and may not be around in another year, my dad could live forever."

"I'm sorry, Robbie. As a friend, I don't agree. When you're on commission, your income comes from your effort. When you own a company, your income comes from all the employees. My dad taught me that. Look at what your family's business has done for your father's net worth. I think you made a short-sighted decision."

"Time will tell. But I'm confident I'll be rich on my own."

CHAPTER 51

The Perfect Type

DAVE PUT ELISA in charge of staffing, recognizing she had many more contacts in the city than he did. Expecting she would hire Tiffany, she surprised him and brought in a woman named Elaine (Lainey) Thompson. When asked about her decision, she said, "Tiffany is looking for a husband. Lainey is looking for a challenge. She's smart and she will contribute to our success."

Elisa also brought in two freelance art directors, explaining that she didn't want to increase overhead too quickly. She also thought it best to use them on a trial basis initially.

She and Dave often worked well into the evening, after starting as early as seven a.m. At the end of a particularly long day, Elisa was reviewing an ad that Dave had completed. Once again, she faulted the typesetting and the type layout within the ad.

Dropping it on Dave's desk, she said, "This is not acceptable. We talked about this back at DBB. You've got to do a better job of type design. It's important to make the type an integral part of the ad, not an appendage."

"Stop being so critical. The ad looks great. Look at that photo."

"That's your problem. You're focused on the image."

"I'm not convinced. It's a terrific ad."

"You're a paradox. You can set up a photo and compose it to make a glass of water look appetizing, and then you design a sloppy ad."

"There isn't time to make it perfect. We're slammed with work, and you're looking for perfection."

"If that's your attitude, then I'm out of here. If we're going to be successful, we have to be better than the competition. That means perfect. Every time. I'm not going to invest my sweat and my reputation on 'pretty good' advertising. So, what's it going to be? I'm serious."

"I want our work to be the best, but it takes me too much time to constantly rework the type to get to that last percentile of perfection that you will accept."

"Okay, then here's a solution. You are brilliant at coming up with breakthrough concepts. Going forward, you develop the advertising concepts and I'll produce the actual ads, or have one of the other art directors do them. Deal?"

"Yes. That will work. I like your solution. We both know typesetting is my weakness."

Dave admitted to himself that it was a good solution, but it wasn't easy dealing with her. Elisa was just as tough as him, as they were both alpha personalities. *The friction will always be there, and she never quits until she wins.*

CHAPTER 52

Delivering on the Promise

AFTER A BLISTERING MONTH of ad production and placement, Lainey walked into Dave's office and announced that the agency billed over $100,000 for the month, including media commissions. He and Elisa, who was at his desk, both looked up and were surprised at the jump in revenue.

Elisa knew they had to add more staff. She also suggested to Dave that they look for a good freelance copywriter. As Lainey was leaving for the weekend, Elisa asked her, "Can you still handle your workload alone, or do you need some help?"

"I'm still getting everything done on time, but if we add any more clients, we'll need a bookkeeper."

"Good. Let me know before you get buried."

Exhausted, Dave and Elisa shut down the office and left the building. Out on the street, he said to her, "How about we get together for dinner tomorrow night and celebrate this billing milestone?"

"Sure. It will give us some quiet time to evaluate our entire operation and make some longer-term plans."

☀ ☀ ☀

Since it was a special evening, Dave took her to the 21 Club. He wore a suit and tie, and Elisa wore a tailored lavender suit with a purple blouse. She looked beautiful. Knowing her penchant for maintaining their business relationship, he refrained from commenting, but he couldn't take his eyes off her.

They started with champagne and their famous Caesar salad. Elisa kicked off the conversation about structuring the agency for the expected growth. She had prepared a note with a schedule and names for full-time staff, and another one for freelance and part-time staff.

While they ate their steaks, Dave said, "As we build up the creative staff, I'd like you to spend more time with me on account service and new business. Clients like having someone attractive on the team, so let's show off your brains *and* beauty. And before you smack me with your handbag, I'm not being a chauvinist—just realistic. Both men and women want to see a good-looking woman in a key position."

"I know what you're saying, but please don't think of me as a sex object."

"I don't, but I want to take advantage of all your assets."

"Yes, I hear what you're saying. It doesn't make me feel comfortable, but it is a fact of life."

"Given that, can you comfortably manage the ad production, public relations, media placement, and administration?"

Smiling, she answered, "With one hand tied behind my back. You already knew you hired the best."

"Then let me make my proposal. When I offered you a position with my imaginary ad agency, I said it would become a partnership. We've worked together for a few months without a hint of disagreement, but that's because I'm subservient to your dictatorial management style." He said it with a broad smile.

With eyes widening, she replied, "What? If you think my pampered treatment of you is dictatorial, then you've led a sheltered life."

"Elisa, you have no idea how traumatic my life has been. But it pales compared to your brutal treatment of me."

"Okay, stop it, you crybaby. You mentioned a partnership."

"Now that the agency has some substance, will you accept my offer for a partnership?"

With an unconvincing frown, she said, "That depends on the percentage."

"I was thinking in the neighborhood of 50 percent."

"That's a nice neighborhood. I accept."

"Hold on. There is a caveat."

"What? You never mentioned anything about a caveat. What is it?"

"I'm the senior partner."

"Fifty percent doesn't make you senior. It makes you equal. Now get used to it. By the way, how big do you think we'll get?"

"Not too big. I never wanted to be really rich because I want to enjoy my life and not be a slave to the business."

"I agree with your philosophy."

"You agree? That's a first."

With a smile, she kicked him under the table.

They enjoyed the remainder of the evening, basking in their success and their consummated deal. Dave told Elisa to put the tab on her expense account since she was now a partner.

They took a cab to her place, and before he got a chance to comment, Elisa said, "No, you're not invited up."

"I had no plans to ask."

She said, "The one thing I like about you is you're easy to train." She leaned over and kissed him on the cheek, adding, "Thank you for everything. I'm even starting to like working with you, except when you select type fonts."

"Me, too. And I'm glad I'm done with type."

Riding in the cab across town to his hotel, he thought, *I wish it could be a romantic relationship. It would be so great.* And as he got out of the cab and looked up at his building, he promised himself he would start to look for an apartment.

CHAPTER 53

Reinforcing the Boundaries

On MONDAY MORNING, Elisa arrived at 7:30 as usual and greeted Dave who was in before six. He told her to get settled and come into his office. When she walked in, he told her to close the door.

"Why?" she asked, "There's no one here."

"I don't even want the mice to hear this conversation. I spent the whole weekend thinking about us, my living situation, and our working together."

Getting nervous, she asked, "You were thinking about us? What's there about us to think about?"

"After dwelling on this for 48 hours, I still don't know how to broach it. Let me make a few statements and, after you agree, I'll offer a plan. There's an elephant in the room. We work very well together, and we are about to be wildly successful. I make you nervous because you expect I'm going to want to start dating, and I don't understand why you're so afraid of a romantic relationship with me. I'm a really good catch." With a smirk, he added, "Even Tiffany would drop everything to date me."

Elisa smiled. "Yes, I am fearful of getting involved with you personally. We have something special here, but we can't live and work together. Both will fail. I chose to work with you, so the rest is off the table."

"You are maddening. Where's your sense of adventure?"

"It's protected by my sense of logic. Do you want to gamble the success of this company for a little sex?"

"Who said anything about sex? I'm looking at a love relationship here. I want to be with you."

"This is what I've been dreading, and you knew it. I do care about you, Dave, and under different circumstances I could fall in love with you. But I can't do this. I'm sorry."

Now with a serious look, Dave said, "Unfortunately, because you're so disciplined, it's what I expected you to say. So, I had to come up with a backup plan."

"Why do you need a plan? Why can't we keep going the way we are? We're doing great."

"Confession time. I'm very lonely. Both my parents died tragically, and there is no one in my life. I need a relationship, and I'm not saying that to put pressure on you."

"You never told me about your parents. That sounds awful. What happened to them?"

"Those are two stories for another day. Sometime in the future, we'll each share our life history. I'd like to know yours." Dave smiled. "Now that you have unceremoniously slammed the door in my face, bruising my perfect Roman nose, I have to move on."

"What do you mean? You're closing the agency?"

"No, not at all. I'm going to find an apartment and move out of my hotel room. And I'm going to start dating."

"Sure. Good luck with the dating scene. What else do we have to discuss?"

"Nothing. Just don't get jealous when I score with some hot babe, and she falls in love with me." Seeing the apprehension growing on her face, he added, "Oh, forget it. Get out of here so I can get some work done."

Walking back to her office, Elisa was relieved. She knew this topic had to come up sooner or later, and she had dreaded it. *He made his case and he backed off. I respect that. I'm so afraid of ruining what we have, and yet, I appreciate that he respects my boundaries. It says a lot about his character.*

The exchange frustrated Dave, but he also did not want to destroy the special relationship they shared. *She made her wishes clear. I have to go in a different direction, but I'm so afraid that it will kill our partnership.*

CHAPTER 54

A New Profit Center

"**D**AVE, IT'S ROBBIE. Would you be interested in handling some brochure work?"

"Sure, we can do brochures and flyers. We just haven't pushed it. Why? What's up"

"I have a client that needs a brochure produced. It needs copywriting, photography, and design. I'll get it printed."

"Bring it over, and we'll get it done. Do you need an estimate?"

"I'll stop by after lunch with the material I have, and you can prepare a quote. We should talk about producing collateral. It could be a big profit center."

"Good idea. I'll have Elisa sit in on the meeting."

When Robbie came in, they met in the conference room and he explained the project for his law firm client. They asked him a few questions and put together an estimate. Robbie then led a discussion about the opportunities he had for producing collateral material, including brochures, posters, displays, packaging, direct mail pieces, and more.

Dave responded that they were eager to add that type of work to their repertoire.

Elisa nodded. "One of our art directors had lots of that experience at a design studio where he worked." She then went out to the bullpen and brought him in to meet Robbie.

Excited about the additional business he could bring to the agency and the resulting commissions, Robbie left, promising to be back with a steady supply of collateral projects.

Afterward, Elisa said to Dave, "I know he brings in a lot of business, but I dislike him. He's always staring at my boobs, tiny as they are. And when you walked out, he hit on me. Does he think every woman is dying to get in bed with him? Please talk to him. Otherwise, I refuse to be in the same room with him."

"Yes, I will. I need you both in these meetings."

CHAPTER 55

An Offer You Can't Refuse

OVER THE NEXT MONTH, Robbie brought collateral projects from 14 different clients. One was for an annual report, but most of the others had an ongoing need for printed material.

Robbie called Dave late one afternoon to tell him he decided to return to his family's printing company.

"That's great news, Robbie. It's a smart decision. What brought it about?"

"My father is dying of pancreatic cancer and the firm needs me. We're meeting next week to work out the details. I don't have much choice, but I am excited about it."

"That is so sad. I respect Papa Joe. He treated me like family. But regardless, I'm glad you're going back. We'll get together for dinner one night soon."

"Yes, as soon as I'm settled. And it won't affect the business I bring to you. That extra income is certainly appreciated."

Jimmy Jones called Dave about a week later to get together for lunch. They met at McSorley's and, after a couple of beers and corned beef sandwiches, Jones told him the news. "We're adding eight new magazines to our portfolio immediately."

"Jimmy, that sounds ambitious. Do you have the staff to manage it?"

"I've doubled my production team and support staff, but most of the writers are freelance. I have a huge stable of them."

"But what about working capital? Can you fund that much expansion so quickly?"

"Here's the good news. We're going public. I have an underwriter, and he's putting together the deal. I'll let you know when we're filing so you can buy some stock. It will take off like a rocket."

"Well, that is exciting. If the new publications are like the existing ones, you can't miss."

Jimmy then asked, "Can your shop handle the added business?"

"If you plan to have similar budgets, I'll need to staff up further. Should I start hiring now?"

"Yes. It will happen fast. And the ad budgets will be at least 25 percent larger for each magazine. I'll have the money, and I want the circulation to jump quickly. That will make the stock price soar. And the price jump will put me in a position to buy other magazine companies. I want to be the McGraw-Hill of sports magazines."

"I'll sit with Elise and figure out what departments we will need to add support staff."

Dave couldn't wait to get back to the office to tell Elisa, but instead of being excited, she got nervous. "This will immediately double our business, and that means much more staffing and added office space. That's going to take a lot of working capital."

"Don't worry about the money. I can finance the growth. Can you recruit enough people that measure up? We're going to need a lot more talent."

"I can start locating the creative people, but I may not be able to do it fast enough. We'll have to use mostly freelancers until we can find the right talent. Support staff is easier. And you're sure you can personally finance this much growth?"

"Yes. I have my father's estate in an offshore account. You had your chance, but now my new girlfriend will get to spend the money."

He detected a slight flinch, but she covered it with a smile and said, "You have a new girlfriend?"

"Not yet, but I expect to find one soon. I've been hanging out at McSorley's."

Laughing, she said, "McSorley's? That's a beer joint full of old relics nursing stale beer."

"Yup. And those are my kind of women."

"Seriously, this new block of business from Jones is troubling me. It's too much at once and it can hurt us. I'm not comfortable with it."

"We'll be fine. Jones always pays on time. He's solid."

CHAPTER 56

Room for Expansion

A NEW TENANT had taken two lower floors in the building. It was a die-cutting and stamping facility using enormous high-speed machines. They began moving in lots of heavy equipment, tying up traffic on the street as the sections were hoisted off flatbed trailers.

Dave called the landlord, concerned about the potential noise from those machines. The owner assured him that the equipment would not be heard on his floor or disturb his staff. While on the phone, Dave inquired about additional space on his floor.

The property owner was excited that Dave needed more space. Except for the remaining footage on the top floor, the building was now fully rented. He made an exceptional offer if Dave took the entire floor on a longer-term lease. It was a lot more than they needed, but it was a good deal and they would likely grow into it in a couple of years.

Dave called Rich Guerrero and had him transfer $200,000 into the company account. Guerrero questioned him, asking about the large amount, and inquiring about their finances.

"Business is already better than we dreamed when we launched it," Dave told him. "We're making money and growing at a rapid pace. That's why we need more working capital."

"I'm delighted for you. Stay in touch. Just don't grow too fast and

195 SISTI | 195

get past yourself. And if you'd like, send me your financials and I'll review them for you."

Dave appreciated the offer. "Thank you, I will send them right away. Reading spreadsheets is one of my weaknesses."

The flood of new work started pouring in, and it kept the growing staff putting in long hours. As the agency was working on all the creative, Jones told Dave their public offering would be completed in forty-five to sixty days. Dave felt reassured by the news, as the billing was skyrocketing.

Elisa and Dave were working long into the night every day to keep up with the volume. The two of them even came in most Saturdays just to clear off their desks and catch up with paperwork.

While Dave wanted to search for an apartment, he was too tired to begin the task. He was relieved when one of the vendors told him about a furnished sub-lease that was available for a six-month rental. Dave took the one-bedroom unit on the upper east side and quickly moved in. He was now ready to get into dating, if he could find the time.

CHAPTER 57

The Hook-up

IT HAD BEEN a few weeks since he spoke to Robbie, and Dave wanted to tell him about his new apartment. When he called, he got his answering machine and left a message to get together for dinner.

After another busy week, Dave decided to take the weekend off and explore his new neighborhood. On Saturday night, he stopped in a local bar and met three attractive women having drinks.

Getting into a casual conversation with them, one woman named Jackie seemed especially friendly. After another round of drinks, the other two said they were leaving and asked Jackie if she was going with them. She said, "No. I'm going to stay a while longer."

Now that they were alone, the conversation got more personal. They talked about jobs, travel, and living in the city. He told her, "I recently moved into the neighborhood on a short-term lease and I'm not familiar with what it offers."

She said, "I could show you around. There are some great places and a few hidden gems here."

"That would be fun. Want to get together tomorrow about three?"

"Sure, that works for me."

"I'm about ready to head back to my place. It's been a tough week. Are you ready to leave, or are you going to stay?"

"No, I'm done. Why don't you walk me home? I'm only two blocks from here, and we can meet in front of my place tomorrow."

Dave walked her to her building, and she reached up and kissed him lightly, saying "Thanks for the drinks. I'm looking forward to tomorrow."

"So am I. See you at three."

The next day they toured the area. Jackie showed him the best dry cleaner, her favorite deli, coffee shop, and grocery store. They walked over to the East River and strolled through the park along the river. She then asked, "Have you ever been to the Gordian Knot?"

"I've never heard of it. Is it a bar?"

"It's the new hot spot here, and they have pretty good seafood."

"Let's go over, have a drink and some dinner."

Even though it was early Sunday evening, the place was packed. They had a cocktail at the bar and when a table was available, they sat down to order a light dinner.

Pure energy, Jackie was the type of person who had to fill every break in the conversation with chatter. It worked well most of the time, as Dave was a little uncomfortable in this dating role. After a few hours, though, it became tiring.

After dinner, they walked back to her place, and she invited him up to see her apartment. It was a cluttered and disorganized one-bedroom with a small living room and galley kitchen. Mimicking Jackie's personality, her selection of furniture and accessories appeared to be the result of impulsive shopping.

She offered him a drink, which he turned down, and thanked him for the afternoon and dinner. Standing close, she put her arms around his neck and kissed him. He responded, extending the kiss as she opened her mouth. She wrapped her arms around his waist and pulled him in closer, pressing her firm breasts against him.

Taking his hand, she brought him into the bedroom and started unbuttoning his shirt. As he undressed, he watched her do the same.

The sex was a little clumsy, despite her leading the way. Afterward, he lay there thinking this wasn't such a good idea after all. She began jabbering, and after about 15 minutes of that, he got up to leave.

"When will I see you again?" she asked.

"Oh, I'll be around, but I'm very busy at work. This is the first weekend I took off in six months." He kissed her and left.

Walking home, he felt like it had been too much work for too little enjoyment. He wasn't happy about the indiscriminate sex. *I feel bad that she's expecting future dates. I've got to be more careful about who I sleep with until I have feelings for the person.*

CHAPTER 58

Devastating News

WHEN ELISA CAME in the next morning, she asked him how he spent his weekend off.

"I had a date and explored my new neighborhood," he told her "What did you do?"

His response triggered a brief pained expression, but she quickly recovered. "Nothing as exciting as your weekend. I cleaned my apartment."

"Who said my weekend was exciting?"

"Well, you had a date. How bad could that be?"

"I met someone at a bar, who spent Sunday afternoon with me and showed me around the neighborhood. She turned out to be a non-stop chatterbox, filling every quiet second with pablum. I think she's president of the 'Stamp Out Silence' association. So it got stale quickly."

"Did you at least get lucky after all that pain? Or can't I ask?"

"Yes, mother. I slept with her. But it won't happen again, I promise."

Elisa laughed, but Dave could see she was troubled by the revelation. "That's too bad since it was your first date in a long time. Maybe next week's offering will be hotter."

"I wasn't kidding when I said it won't happen again. It's too big a step to engage in frivolously."

Elisa smiled. "That's very mature coming from a man. They all look at sex as detached fun with no emotional consequences. I'm beginning to like you."

"I doubt that. Now get out of here and do some work."

Later in the day, Dave got a phone call. "Dave, it's Shelly Sutrina. You probably don't remember me, but I'm Robbie's wife."

"Of course I remember you. We had dinner together. I've been trying to reach Robbie. Is everything okay?"

"Actually, no. That's why I'm calling. I found your message on his home business phone and wanted to call you back. Robbie was killed on a street corner in Greenwich Village a couple of weeks ago. There's an investigation, so I still don't know the details. He was shot in the head during a robbery."

"Oh, Shelly, that's horrible! Is there anything I can do?"

"Thank you, no. I'm fine. But I thought you needed to know. Bye, now."

Dave sat and stared at the phone. He was shocked by the news and couldn't believe Shelly's cold, detached demeanor. Choking back tears at the loss of his friend, he thought, *Will this terrible city ever stop taking the good people?*

CHAPTER 59

Unexpected Delay

ALL THE MAGAZINE ADS for Jones' publications had been placed the previous month to meet the print deadlines, and now the rest of the massive campaign was taking place. It was all timed to coordinate with the launch date of the public offering. Jimmy Jones was certain all this advertising and its publicity would have a residual benefit and drive up the share price.

Dave had opened an account at Merrill Lynch so he could invest in Outdoor Sports Publications, Inc. when it went public. He instructed his new broker to buy $10,000 in shares on the scheduled opening date.

On the morning of the launch, Dave's stockbroker called to tell him the SEC had held up the offering because of a problem with the underwriting. When asked how long the delay would take, he answered, "It could be a week, but more likely a few months. The SEC is very careful about these situations. Their job is to protect investors from unscrupulous predators in the market."

When Dave called Jones, only to find his client wasn't in the office, he became worried. Although Outdoor Sports was directly responsible for the massive media bills from the TV stations and magazines, the agency hadn't been paid for any of the creative or production work, and those costs were staggering.

He called Elisa and the management team into the conference

room and told them about the potential problem. "We're looking at a delay in payment from Outdoor Sports. There's a glitch in the stock launch and the SEC is holding it up."

Elisa said, "I've been concerned about this project from the beginning. Is there any chance the company won't go public?"

Dave answered with a little trepidation. "I doubt it, but anything can happen. I'll know better when I talk to Jimmy. But assuming it does go through, we may have to wait a few months before we get paid."

The bookkeeper said everything for the campaign was billed, and the total was nearly one million dollars.

"Can we stop the orders on any of the components of the campaign?" Dave asked.

Lainey shook her head. "No. Everything is out. The mailings were scheduled to be complete last week, and all the advertising is running now. We can't stop any of it."

Dave said, "Then all we can do now is wait to hear from Jimmy. I'll keep trying him, but we may be in serious trouble."

As the meeting broke up, he saw the look on Elisa's face and knew what she was thinking. *Impending disaster is on our doorstep.*

CHAPTER 60

Financial Limbo

JONES FINALLY CALLED back at five o'clock that evening. He hadn't been able to get in touch with the underwriter, but he called the SEC and was told that the filing fee hadn't been received by them. There were also errors and inconsistencies in the original application request.

Noting that the issues were minor, he told Dave not to worry as he would have the problem solved within a week. "If it goes much past that, we're all fucked," he said. "But trust me, I won't let that happen."

Dave again called the team into the conference room. He told them about his conversation with Jones and said, "Jimmy is a pretty savvy businessman. I've got a lot of confidence in him. This glitch doesn't seem to be anything serious, and he's certain it will be resolved in a week. The missing filing fee is about $5,000, so that's not a deal-breaker."

Elisa asked, "What's the worst-case scenario if this whole thing implodes?"

"That's why I called you all in. We've got to be prepared."

The bookkeeper again mentioned the one million dollars outstanding, including the anticipated media commissions that might be defaulted.

Lainey chimed in, "That's the potential financial loss, but we must consider the overhead. We signed a long-term lease for the entire floor, we built out all the new offices and upgraded them with new furniture and we've tripled our staff. All the costs associated with that could come back to bite us."

Dave added, "Without Robbie, new business is certain to slow down substantially."

The conversation continued for another hour, which included a discussion about how to pare the staff if necessary. Finally, Dave said, "Okay everybody, go home. We know what we're up against and we're helpless to control it right now. Let's hope Jimmy comes through."

Everyone left in a funk, coming down from the euphoria of the past few months. Dave stayed behind and called Guerrero. He told him about their predicament and asked for his advice.

Rich said, "Dave, sometimes no matter how careful you are, you will still get hurt. Wait until you get confirmation from your client and then we can plan your solution. If the publisher goes down, you will have to decide if you have enough remaining business to survive."

"Send me another hundred thousand to stay afloat until I know where we stand. It will take a lot of cash to continue the business without the magazine publisher. Do I have enough funds in my account?"

"We'll have to look at your financial situation at that time, but it could get close to wiping you out. Have your bookkeeper send me financial statements and projections as of today, and prepare another set, after you determine the viability of your client."

The next call he made was to Papa Joe. He hadn't spoken to him in a while, and after Shelly's call, he wanted to find out more about what happened to Robbie. Despite sounding weak, Papa Joe was delighted to hear from him. "Dave, how are you doing? Business okay?"

"Actually, it's not. But that isn't why I called. What happened to Robbie? And how are you holding up?"

"I'm struggling with the cancer treatments, and Robbie's passing has only made it worse."

"Shelly called me and couldn't give me any details. What did happen?"

"Robbie was on his way to the shop to sign the deal we worked out to bring him back. We had a celebration set up for his return, and he never showed up."

"That sounds awful."

"It gets worse. Apparently, he stopped at a bar for a drink on his way here and was in a conversation with some drifter in the bar. Robbie left and then the drifter left. They found him behind the bar, robbed and shot in the head. The police are still looking for the drifter to see if he's connected."

CHAPTER 61

The Attack

DAVE WALKED HOME in the dark, stopping to get a hotdog from a street vendor. He was weighing his options, trying to determine what remaining business he had if the magazine account went down.

He took into consideration Robbie's shocking death and how that would affect future sales. He was certain that a portion of those clients would begin to depart without Robbie's effort. And of course, there would never be any new business coming from him.

He concluded that it would be extremely difficult to survive with their high overhead. Recognizing how critical Robbie had been to their success, he knew he faced a bleak outlook for maintaining and building the client base. He would discuss it with Elisa in the morning.

Meanwhile, further downtown, Elisa was walking down Second Avenue and when she turned onto 55th Street, someone came up behind her and shoved her into the wall of an apartment building. The impact knocked the wind out of her. As she turned to scream, her attacker punched her in the face, then hit her a few more times. When she crumpled to the ground, he grabbed her purse, ran to the corner, and was gone.

Crying and in pain, she staggered the rest of the way to her building and went up to her apartment. Stripping down, she took a hot washcloth and wiped off the blood and grime. Elisa then checked the bones around her face and head to confirm nothing was broken.

Wrapping some ice cubes in the washcloth and holding it against her cheekbone, she called Dave. The call went to his answering machine, and when she started to speak, she started sobbing and hung up.

When Dave walked into his apartment, he saw the message light flashing on the phone and heard Elisa crying. Alarmed, he called immediately. "Hey, what happened?"

"Oh, Dave. I was attacked right down the street from my apartment. He beat me up and stole my purse. Fortunately, I had my keys in my hand. It's an old habit." She started to cry again.

"How bad are you hurt? Do you want me to take you to the hospital? Did you call the police?"

"I'll be alright. I'm icing the bruises and I'm sore as hell. And no. I didn't even think of calling the cops."

"Call them right away. He's got your address. He could come back and rob you again in your apartment. Why don't I come down and bring you some dinner? I can stay with you tonight, so you're not alone."

"I'll call them now. But don't come here. I'm not hungry, and I can't have you see me looking like this."

"What? You're letting vanity drive your decisions? You need someone with you. You should listen to the trauma in your voice. I'm coming over, and don't bother to put on any makeup."

CHAPTER 62

Comfort and Compassion

GRABBING A BOTTLE of wine from his cabinet, Dave raced out the door. When he got to her neighborhood, he stopped at a neighborhood Italian restaurant and bought some pasta and meatballs.

It took him less than an hour to get there. Elisa answered the door wearing sweats. She had cleaned up her face and combed her hair but, as ordered, wore no makeup.

"Come in and don't look at me."

Relieved at how she looked and sounded, he said, "The bruised look adds character to your face. You should make it a permanent feature."

"Keep it up, smartass, and you'll be sporting the same look."

He reached out and gently hugged her. "Fortunately, you're one tough broad. You'll be fine." He continued to hold her as she pulled him in tighter and began to quietly sob.

As Elisa heated the food, Dave opened the wine and looked around the apartment. It had two bedrooms, a large living room, and a small, open kitchen with a table for two. He was impressed with how beautifully she had decorated the living room with original art on the walls and an expensive sofa, two plush chairs, and a set of occasional tables.

They shared the food, with Dave eating most of it. Elisa didn't have much of an appetite, but they did finish the bottle of wine.

A while later, two police officers arrived at the door. Elisa invited them in and introduced Dave. They all sat in the living room, with the officers taking the two chairs while Elisa and Dave sat on the couch. She took his hand and held it.

The younger officer had a notebook, and they went through the questions on his form. When asked, she said, "It was dark, and I couldn't get a good look at him."

Then the older one asked if Elisa wanted to go to the hospital. When she shook her head they stood and told her there wasn't much chance of capturing the perp, but she should come to the station the next week and pick up a copy of the crime report for her insurance company. They also advised her to call her credit card companies.

After the police left, Dave said, "You get ready for bed. I'm not leaving you alone tonight."

"No. It's okay. I'll be fine" she said, as she squeezed back tears.

"Look at you. You're not okay. I'm staying. I'll sleep on the couch. You get to bed. Now." He said it with such authority, she didn't argue.

Elisa went into the bedroom and put on a nightgown. She picked a plain ankle-length gown, brushed her teeth, and brought a pillow and blanket to Dave. He had tossed his clothes on the chair and was lying on the couch in his underwear.

When he saw her nightgown, he said, "Was that your grandmother's?"

They both laughed and she answered, "It's how I feel right now."

"Get in your room and get some sleep. You'll feel better tomorrow, but tonight will be difficult."

Dave lay there thinking about her horrible experience. It pained him to see how much she hurt, both from the beating and the emotional toll. He hoped his presence in the apartment would help calm her, but he knew she would struggle to fall asleep.

Elisa also lay awake in her bed, unable to get the attack out of her head. Despite claiming she would be all right, she was glad Dave had stayed. She realized she needed the comfort of him being close by.

After tossing for about an hour, exhaustion took over and she fell into a restless sleep. A couple of hours later, she had a nightmare about the attack and cried out. Dave came running into the bedroom and found her covered with sweat and shaking. He kissed her on the forehead and went into the bathroom for a towel.

After he patted her down, he said, "I'm going to sleep next to you. It may help. And I promise I'll behave."

She nodded and murmured, "Thank you, please do."

He got his pillow and lay next to her, taking her hand. She seemed to relax, and her breathing became steady. After a while, she turned to him and lay on her side, putting her arm across his chest. She soon fell back asleep, as did Dave.

Toward morning, he awoke to her touch as her leg was over his thighs and she was gently caressing his chest. He turned to her and pulled her in close. Elisa was aroused and began rubbing her abdomen against his. Dave whispered, "Are you sure you want to do this? I can't do it unless you're comfortable with it."

She didn't answer but rubbed harder and leaned up and kissed him. He took that as tacit approval. The lovemaking was slow and sweet. Afterward, she fell back asleep in his arms. He lay there in a blissful state and did not experience that feeling of regret he had with Jackie.

CHAPTER 63

No More Boundaries

DAVE AWOKE at six and took a shower. He used Elisa's toothbrush, pleased that there wasn't an extra toothbrush for guests. He got dressed and made a pot of coffee. Sitting in the kitchen, he called his credit card company, canceled Elisa's corporate card, and ordered a replacement.

About seven-thirty, Elisa dragged herself into the kitchen and poured a cup of coffee. She sat across from Dave, looking down. When she finally raised her eyes to him, she said, "Thank you for being here for me. I don't know how I would have gotten through the night without you. It's morning and I don't hate you."

"I was worried about that. Our relationship is too important to be crushed by sex."

"It wasn't sex. It was lovemaking and I initiated it. And just as you explained how you felt after your recent encounter, it can't be casual for me either."

He reached across the table and squeezed her hand. "You have no idea how difficult it is for me not to hug you every time I see you, but my self-control has held up very well."

"I know. You were ready to stop me last night. That confirmed the kind of person you are, and I'm so glad we didn't stop."

Dave grinned. "So, this wasn't an example of 'extreme trauma sex'?"

"No. It was gentle lovemaking, and did I ever need it." She stroked his hand.

"We now have to figure out where we go from here, and that includes us and the business. I must get to the office. You stay home and call your credit card companies. I already called to have your corporate card replaced. I'll be back tonight with dinner, and we'll talk then."

When he got to the office, Dave called the staff into a meeting and told them about Elisa's mugging. He explained that she was heavily bruised and would be out for a few days, but she was okay. He warned everyone to be careful, as this was the second attack in the city that affected him personally in the past few weeks.

Dave's first call was to Jimmy Jones but, when he was unable to reach him, he left an urgent message. He was becoming certain that a major disaster was in the making on this account, but he had no idea how to address it.

CHAPTER 64

Contingency Plan

ON HIS WAY to Elisa's after work, Dave stopped at a Jewish deli and bought chicken soup, brisket, and a couple of sides, along with a bottle of Valpolicella. He had called her during the day to check up on her. She was feeling better, although she was sore and the bruises were turning blue.

They ate dinner quietly and had their second glass of wine in the living room. Elisa started the conversation by asking, "What's going on at the office?"

"Nothing good. With the magazine campaign crunch behind us and not much in the hopper, we're slowing down. I tried to call Jones, but he didn't return my call. Tomorrow's Friday and if we don't hear from him then, we're doomed."

"Is there any way we can salvage the company?"

"That's all I've been thinking about the last few days. I'm convinced the public offering is not going to happen, but if Jones has the funds to pay for the creative and production, we can make it. Even if he can pay most of it, we'll survive. I can use my money to keep us solvent."

"What's the worst case?"

"If Jones is stretched out from launching the new magazines and financing the underwriting costs for the offering, he'll go bankrupt. With our high overhead, we'll be right behind him."

"Isn't there any way we can continue without him?"

"We will have lost all the magazine business, and with Robbie's death, we have no rainmaker. He represented a lot of new business, mostly small projects, but very profitable. We have now more than doubled our overhead and drained our cash on the office expansion, plus all the money we paid out for the magazine campaign. We will be toast."

"Oh, Dave, what will we do? We'll have to get jobs somewhere."

"I'm glad you said *we*. Because that's the direction I'm taking. I'm thinking us."

"Yes, so am I. So, tell me what you have in mind."

"It's a radical plan, but let me describe it and then I'll share the rationale. We'll probably have to bankrupt the company. I may also have to file for personal bankruptcy, as I had to sign the lease personally and that, cumulatively, is over four hundred thousand. Either way, we move to New Jersey, rent an apartment, and open a small promotional agency."

"Wow, that is radical, but tell me why. I'm not convinced, but I'm not ruling it out either."

"I'm done with New York. When I was a kid, we lived in a brownstone, not far from this apartment. My dad and I returned from a vacation trip in the Adirondacks to find my mother raped and murdered and our house robbed. My friend Robbie was just killed behind a bar. He was robbed, as well. And now, you get beat up and have your purse stolen. That's reason enough to get out of this crime-infested city.

"I didn't know about your mother. I can't imagine how tragic that must have been. I understand why you want to move, but how will we survive a new business launch?"

"I'm confident we can hold onto a few accounts. I have enough cash to keep us solvent until we develop some additional business."

"The more you talk, the more I realize how little I know about you. How much do you have and where did you get it? If you don't mind me asking."

"After my mother died, my dad sold the brownstone and retired from IBM. He put all of his retirement benefits, as well as the money from the house, into an account in the Bahamas. I don't know exactly what I have left in the account, but it should be less than a million dollars. And I don't mind you asking. I have no secrets and will never keep anything from you."

He then told her about moving to Indian Lake, his father's death, his photography and advertising businesses, and the attempted framing for murder—all occurring while he was in his late teens and early twenties.

Elisa sat there in shock, unable to comprehend how Dave lived through all that without any support or advice. "How were you able to keep your sense of humor and your business mind intact?"

"It has always been my sense of humor that keeps me sane and moving forward."

"You may have that money left in your account. But you should know, I don't have very much—a few thousand dollars is all."

Dave laughed. "That's good because I'm not marrying you for your money."

"Who said anything about marriage?"

"Oh, I thought I wrote that into the partnership agreement."

"No. That would have been a deal killer."

They both started laughing and Elisa reached over and hugged him.

Getting serious, she said, "Let's hang on as long as we can and see if Jones pulls through. Then we can decide on our next move. If it's setting up a new venture in New Jersey, I'm okay with it."

"Even if Image Concepts survives, I'm still considering living across the river. The rents are much lower in New Jersey, and Lainey never stops talking about how beautiful it is in Bergen County."

"Dave, we're now us. I'm with you."

CHAPTER 65

Scrambling to Survive

WHEN DAVE got to the office Friday morning, there was a message recorded from Jones. "The filing got delayed for a few weeks but is still going forward. The underwriter needed additional funding as there were issues with paperwork and regulations."

Jones said he forwarded the money and would call Dave next week with an update.

The phone call was reassuring but not convincing. Dave was still apprehensive. He called Elisa and let her know. She said, "Why don't you plan to stay here at my place this weekend. We still have a lot to talk about."

"I was planning to do that even if we have nothing to talk about."

Given the many challenges facing the agency, Dave itemized the tasks he needed to address. With the Jones problem on hold, his next most critical project was keeping the clients Robbie brought in. He made a list of all those companies and drafted a letter to the CEO of each one of them requesting a meeting in light of Robbie's death.

He then met with the bookkeeper to review the cash flow. She took him through the payables and receivables showing him that everything was current except the massive unpaid invoices due from Jones and corresponding bills to be paid. All the freelancers were paid up to date, which left very little cash in the account. Dave told her he was putting another $100,000 in the checking account the following week to pay any bills that were due.

Lainey came into his office later and asked Dave, "Can you hear that hum? It's something new and it's very annoying."

"I can feel a vibration mostly in the early morning and after hours."

"My office is closer to the elevators and it's much louder there."

"I'll pay closer attention. If it gets worse, I'll have the landlord add some insulation to our walls to deaden the sound. He assured us we wouldn't hear the machines downstairs."

At lunchtime, Dave called Elisa to check in. He told her about his plan to write a letter to Robbie's clients. She liked the idea and said, "Bring home some stationery. I can type the letters here at my desk in the other bedroom."

"You have a desk in the other bedroom? Where am I going to sleep?"

"If you don't behave, it'll be back in your own apartment, wiseass."

"Do you need any groceries? I'm going to stop at a supermarket and make dinner tonight."

"Sounds great. When will you be doing the laundry and vacuuming? Oh, and the ironing's not done."

"And I'm the wiseass?"

She gave him a list of breakfast items and staples and suggested he bring some wine, as well.

CHAPTER 66

Intimate Behavior

Knocking on the door with his foot, Dave showed up with two bags of groceries and a smaller sack holding a few bottles of wine.

Opening the door, she said, "Whoa, are we having a party here tonight?"

"A small intimate party with the emphasis on intimate. I'm making fettuccini alfredo."

They both prepped dinner and sipped white wine. After too much pasta and salad, they sat on the couch, drinking the last dregs from the wine bottle.

Elisa asked, "Anything else happen at work?"

"Let's not talk about work. I want to know more about you, and I'm sure you have a thousand questions about me. We have all weekend to discuss the agency."

"Well, you've already determined that I'm a tough broad. Actually, though, I'm a sweet, demure lady. What else could you possibly want to know?"

"Is there anything about you that I might like?"

"Probably not, but I'll tell you about my background. I was born in Italy and came here with my mom when I was ten. My father had a business in Italy. He was going to sell it and follow us here, but what we didn't know was that he had cancer. He died six months after we left."

"That's sad, but interesting in that we share similar misfortunes."

"For me, it was a disaster. I was his little girl, and he always spoiled me. I felt abandoned, alone in a country where I couldn't speak the language. My mother was angry and bitter, and life was miserable. She worked in a slipper factory, but we had very little money. She never stopped blaming my father for the predicament we were in."

"We lived in Hackensack until she died when I was 19. That's when I moved into the city. I couldn't afford a car back then, and you needed one to get around in New Jersey. New York City offered education, employment, transportation, and energy. I got all four."

"Italy, huh? I often wondered where your heavy accent came from."

"I don't have an accent, but you should talk. Every word you say has a hard consonant. You even add them to words that end in vowels."

"It's ironic that both of us were left on our own at a young age and we managed to survive in pretty good shape. You know about my career path. How did you get started in the ad business?"

Elisa told Dave about getting a job at a typography shop as a secretary where she learned to set type. She then worked as a mechanical artist at a design studio. During that time, she took classes at Pratt, including graphic design courses, and got her degree. She had no social life and just focused on her studies.

"Dating in New York was a nightmare. All every guy wanted to do was get laid, and you never knew which ones were married. The women weren't much better. They thought the road to marriage went through their thighs."

Dave burst out laughing. "For a prude, you've got a good sense of humor."

"Prude? How could you say that? No one is easier than me. Now tell me more about you. I still don't know how you survived all that pain and came out seemingly unscathed."

"I told you, it's my focus. I see the humor in everything. It drives

220 | ON THE BRINK

my creativity and keeps me sane. Also, my father taught me how to be prepared and remain calm in critical situations."

"Okay, no more talk. The wine is getting to me. Let's go to bed."

When they went into the bedroom, Elisa asked, "Do you want to take a shower first?"

"Yes, I'd love one."

She got him a towel and he climbed into the shower stall. After a few minutes, the door opened, and she joined him. They soaped each other down and rinsed off. Before getting out they stood hugging each other under the steady spray of hot water.

As they toweled off, Elisa slipped into a silky, see-through nightie and no underwear. Taking his cue from her, Dave got into bed naked. He told her that was how he always slept.

They kissed, cuddled, and caressed until they were both aroused. The orgasm came with much more energy and speed than the previous night. They continued to hold each other until Elisa fell asleep. Then Dave nodded off.

As usual, he was up before six. He went into the kitchen and made coffee, letting her sleep. They never left the apartment all weekend, making frequent visits to the bedroom. They each thought it was the best weekend of their lives.

CHAPTER 67

A Coffin Nail

Early MONDAY MORNING, Dave left Elisa in bed and went to the office. After her breakfast that morning, she began to type the letters to the clients. By mid-afternoon the letters and envelopes were complete, awaiting Dave's signature and the postage meter stamp. The letters were signed and mailed on Tuesday. She remained home for a few more days until her face healed completely.

The following week, Dave began to call each client. For the smaller accounts with occasional projects, he pitched them over the phone. He stated his commitment to them and asked if there was anything he could do to improve the relationship. Virtually all the responses were positive, and they all told him they would call when they next needed his services.

His calls to the handful of larger clients were to set up appointments to cement a bond with them. They all agreed to meet.

Later in the week, as Dave was working after hours, he noticed that the vibration and noise from the equipment downstairs was getting louder and more intense. Feeling the pronounced movement in the floor under his feet, he called the landlord and complained. He wanted relief from it, reminding the owner that he was assured this would not happen. The landlord reluctantly agreed to add insulation on his floor and would see about the vibration.

Since he hadn't heard back from Jones, Dave called him for an update on the filing. Jones said, "We're doomed. The underwriter was a crook and scammed us. After the public offering date was missed, I paid another twenty-five thousand to get the filing issues resolved. Now I've lost contact with him."

"I can't believe it. That kind of swindle hasn't happened in years."

"It happens more than you think. He conned me and had my trust. I paid out hundreds of thousands of dollars, and all he did was start the filing and never completed it. There will be no public offering."

Dave was crushed. "Is there any way you can stay afloat?"

"No. We used all our available cash and borrowed to the maximum of our credit line to create the eight new magazines. I even took a personal loan against my house. The deal was that good. Now, I'm up to my fat ass in debt with no way out. I'll probably lose the house, as well."

Desperate, Dave asked, "Is there any way you could send us some money? This will wipe us out as well."

"I'm so sorry, Dave. Even if I had it, a bankruptcy judge would claw it back. I owe money to so many creditors."

After he hung up, the reality set in. The agency would fold, and he was personally on the hook for a five-year lease. When he walked into the apartment later that evening, Elisa saw his face and knew immediately that the agency was about to fail.

Holding her in his arms as they sat on the sofa, he shared the details of his conversation with Jones. He then said, "I'm too drained to discuss our next steps. We'll work on it at the office tomorrow. Let's have dinner and go to bed."

Elisa looked into his eyes. "First, I want to say something. Whenever we speak it's either business or banter. I fought the emotion for a long time because you scare me, but I'm so glad we're together. I am in love with you."

Pulling her in tight, he became choked up. "I fell in love with you very early on and I fought it, knowing it was not what you wanted. I am thrilled we're together. And if we go broke, it will be worth it to end up like this with you."

CHAPTER 68

The Final Nail

DAVE LEFT for the office the next morning even earlier than usual. The first thing he saw when he turned onto his street were the flashing lights of police cars and emergency vehicles. He ran up to his building to find the entrance covered with crime-scene tape.

He asked the officer guarding the front entrance what had happened. "We don't know for sure, but we think a steel girder cracked. The night crew that runs the equipment felt the floor shake. They evacuated and called the precinct."

"My office is in this building. Can I go up?"

"Absolutely not. Nobody goes in until the building inspector clears it for occupancy."

A short while later, the inspector arrived with two other men and a uniformed fire official. They looked around the perimeter of the building and went in.

By now the landlord had arrived and was vehemently arguing with the police officer to let him into the building. He was just as vehemently turned down. Dave's staff and the other tenants were gathering in the front, all waiting to go in. Elisa arrived and stood next to Dave.

It was nearly an hour before the inspection crew returned to the street. The landlord ran up to them, introduced himself, and asked when the occupants could go in.

Shaking his head, the inspector addressed everyone in a loud voice to carry out to the large crowd that was gathered in the street. "This building is closed to occupancy until further notice. There is a broken floor beam that has damaged the concrete on the second floor. It is causing the floor to sag. The building is not rated to carry the weight of the equipment that sits on it. The vibration of the running machines made the situation worse."

The landlord spoke up, "You can't arbitrarily close this building indefinitely. We've got to get people back in there."

"This building may never open again."

With that comment, the crowd began to dissipate in shock. Dave told his staff to go home and await a call from him. He then went up to the inspector and asked if he could walk up the stairs and get the bookkeeping ledgers out of his office.

The inspector said, "There's no way anyone is going into this building. It could collapse at any time. We're going to block off this entire area until we take some remedial steps to protect the adjacent buildings."

He and Elisa hung around a while longer, as the emergency vehicles began to leave. One police car remained in front of the building with its lights flashing an officer stationed at the front entrance.

The building next door to them, which was separated by an alley, housed a coffee shop. Dave took Elisa in there and they ordered coffee. It was a gloomy storefront that catered to mostly take-out orders. Sitting at a table near the back, he said, "Wait here. I'm going out the back and see if I can get in our building."

"Are you crazy? Yes, you are crazy. The inspector said the building could collapse at any time. Why do you want to go up there?"

"I don't think I weigh enough to cause the building to collapse. Although, it would be far riskier if I sent you in." That got him a punch on his shoulder. He continued, "We've got to get our books out so we can manage our money. Is there anything up there that you must have?"

"I guess just my Rolodex."

"Okay, I'll get both of ours, the client ledger, and the checkbook."

Dave walked down the back hall, past the restrooms, and out the back door into the alley. Next to the foul-smelling dumpsters, he found a crate that he took with him to the back of his building.

He used the crate to jump up and reach the suspended fire escape ladder and took the fire escape to the top floor. The old wire-glass windows in the back had no locks, and he was able to get in easily. Quickly gathering up the items he needed, he stuffed them in a trash bag he found near the freight elevator. A few minutes later, he was back in the coffee shop.

Elisa said, "I can't believe you pulled that off. I kept listening for the building to implode. Sitting here I was worried for you, but I realized just how important this stuff is. We can't do anything without these records."

"It's critical to us, regardless of what our next steps are. And you can be certain that before the day is out, the city will have hired a security company to guard the building. This was our only shot at getting our books."

CHAPTER 69

Shutting Down

WHEN THEY GOT BACK to the apartment, Dave and Elisa sat at the table and took stock of their situation.

"The two biggest decisions have been made for us," Dave said. "We must file the bankruptcies for the agency and me, and we have to set up shop somewhere else."

"Yes, but do we stay in the city or move to New Jersey?"

"We just lost our biggest client, so nothing is anchoring us here. It's a new beginning, new relationship, and soon a new agency. So let's do it all in a new place."

"I like your rationale. And I'm even starting to like your cute smile."

"The other important consideration, in addition to my cute smile, is New Jersey will be a lot more affordable in every way—rent, taxes, cost of living, and more. Also, staff salaries and freelance rates will be lower there."

"Now that the key decisions are made, let's list our tasks and get started."

As Dave started articulating them, Elisa wrote them down. "Go to the post office and have our mail forwarded here. Call the phone company to install another phone and have the phone lines transferred here. Make appointments to visit every client to explain our situation and potential move. Schedule more frequent sex."

"Wait a minute," Elisa said. "We're already doing it too often."

"Too often? The atrophy is making it difficult for me to perform."

"Given your age, maybe you should start taking Geritol."

"See, you're catching on. Our sense of humor will save us. Now, since we are moving to New Jersey, let's continue with the same company name."

"Is that legal if we file bankruptcy?"

"I think we can incorporate the same name in New Jersey. We also need to decide on a location. Let's spend the weekend exploring Bergen County and narrow down our choices."

"I'll call Lainey and get some ideas from her."

"And confidentially let her know what our plans are. She will probably be the only employee we keep when we start up the new shop."

Dave jumped up and said, "We left Rich Guerrero off the to-do list."

"Who's Rich Gurreror?"

"I thought you were an Italian from Italy. And you can't pronounce a Mediterranean name like Guerrero?"

"I was just trying to say it the way you did."

"You know, when I met you, you were all business. You had a nice wall built around you so no one could get close. I was afraid if you smiled, your face would crack. And now, every other sentence is a poke or a jab. What happened to you?"

"You happened to me," Elisa said. "Yes, I was a reserved lady being reserved and professional. Then I fell in love with this clown, and he made me join the circus."

"Ahh, a circus clown. I'm beginning to see the image you have of me. And in answer to your snide remark about pronunciation, my diction is perfect, just like every other New Yorker. Anyway, he's my banker from the Bahamas."

Dave immediately got him on the phone, "Hi Rich, it's Dave

Powers. Our agency just got hit with a double whammy. We've encountered the two worst possible problems."

"Oh, no. Tell me what's happening."

"As we feared, our biggest client is going bankrupt, so we will lose upwards of a million dollars. And in addition to that, our building has just been condemned due to a major safety issue. So, now we can't even run the business."

"Are you telling me you're locked out of your building? For how long?"

"The building inspector said the building may never open again."

"Actually, that may be good news. Did you use the Stokes Agency for your insurance when you launched the company?"

Confused, Dave said, "Yes, we're using them on your recommendation. But this isn't an insurance issue."

"Of course it is. If Marty Stokes wrote your policies, you have business interruption insurance, you have coverage for your furniture, equipment, etc. You may even have coverage for losses from client bankruptcies."

"I honestly don't know about any of that."

"Also, the landlord must have insurance coverage that you can tap into, particularly if the building is rendered unusable or is destroyed."

"Rich, you have my head spinning. This could make all the difference in the world."

"Call Marty right away and explain your predicament. He was my roommate at NYU, and he'll tell you what options you have. And let me know what you need after that."

Dave quickly shared what he learned from Rich. Then he called Marty Stokes and made an appointment to meet him Monday morning.

During the afternoon, they went to the post office and called the phone company. They decided not to call the clients just yet, though, as the situation was still fluid.

Afterward, they relaxed, took showers, and went to dinner at Smith and Wollensky. During dinner, Elisa said, "This will be our Friday night tradition. Date night every Friday."

Knowing they were both on mental overload, Dave suggested they still go to Bergen County the next day. And during the ride, they could explore all the possible scenarios that any insurance claims could yield.

After dinner, they went home and enjoyed their lovemaking. They fell asleep with the anticipation of the weekend excursion exploring northern New Jersey.

CHAPTER 70

Rescue Plan

ON MONDAY MORNING, Dave and Elisa visited the well-appointed offices of the Stokes Agency in the Graybar Building adjacent to Grand Central Station. Marty Stokes walked out to the reception foyer, greeted them, and brought them into his conference room. He told them, "Rich Guerrero called me over the weekend and advised me of your plight. You can fill me in on the details."

After refusing coffee, Dave explained their two key problems as Stokes listened and took notes. Referring to the file folder he was carrying, Stokes confirmed that they had all the necessary coverage to prevent the demise of the ad agency.

He suggested they start by filing a complaint against the building owner for preventing them from conducting business or even accessing their books and files.

He explained, "The landlord's insurance will not consider any claims until the building's survival is determined."

Dave commented, "But that could take a year or more."

"Yes, but at the same time you can file claims through your own coverage, as they will provide funds more quickly. They will also likely assist you in going after the landlord's insurer."

"If the building gets demolished, you are covered for all your contents," he explained. "And you do have coverage for business interruption plus losses from client non-payment, but it doesn't cover

100 percent of the loss. There's a big deductible on the non-payment reimbursement."

Dave's mind was running in multiple directions at the same time. An idea was forming in his head, but he didn't want to discuss it with Stokes.

"This is far better than we expected," he said. "We will file the claims as soon as we can prepare the documents. Let's see where it takes us."

After they left Stokes' office and got in a cab, Elisa said, "Okay, I can see the smoke coming out of your ears and that nutty professor look in your eyes. You've already come up with a solution and probably an entirely different plan. So, let's hear it."

"It's only a modification of our plan. The insurance money is our savior. Our ad agency doesn't have to file bankruptcy, and neither do I. The lease becomes invalid, so I'm off the hook. And we can collect enough from either our insurance company or the landlord's—or both—to get most of our bills paid. This avoids the agency going under."

"Okay, so then what? Where do we go?"

"I'm still committed to moving to New Jersey. We keep the agency intact, except we lay off the staff. We find a suitable location in Bergen County and resume on a smaller scale, as we will have far less business than we had up until now. And we no longer have Robbie."

"You're right. That will work. I knew you had one redeeming quality."

"And that's why you're sticking with me?"

"No, it's the sex."

Escaping the Concrete Jungle

CHAPTER 71

Image Concepts Lite

DAVE AND ELISA were in their new offices ready to launch the next chapter of their adventure. They had rented space in an office building on Route 4 in Paramus, New Jersey, less than ten miles from New York City via the George Washington Bridge. That was a key selling point for leasing this particular space. They wanted their New York clients to know they were only fifteen minutes from the city.

It was a new building, and they reserved 1,000 square feet with room for expansion. Elisa picked out the furniture, which consisted of primarily modular office partitions with built-in desks and cabinets in an open floor plan with a sleek contemporary look.

When they started their search, Lainey had suggested the Paramus area. Elisa also thought this centrally located town, intersected by two major highways, would be their best bet. She did not want to return to Hackensack, where she had many bad memories.

It had been a whirlwind four months since they were locked out of the damaged building that housed their business in New York. Between that and their largest client's demise, they struggled to survive.

Fortunately, the shutdown of their building in New York enabled Dave to walk away from that huge lease, and the insurance money enabled them to pay down most of the agency's bills. The money

Dave had drawn from his bank account at the time more than covered the rest.

During that period, the building was condemned and scheduled for demolition. All their office furniture, typewriters, and drafting tables were lost as the building was inaccessible. Since Elisa's extra bedroom had been furnished as an office, they purchased two drafting tables and continued to produce work for their remaining clients until they could get set up in New Jersey.

Dave and Elisa had visited every client and explained their plight, asking each one to remain with them as they transitioned to a new location. Although a few of their clients agreed to continue their existing campaigns, most decided to wait until Image Concepts was reestablished before making any commitments with them.

Their relocated agency opened for business in Paramus under the same name. Using the slogan *The New York agency without the New York Attitude*, they hoped to rekindle the accounts they had when they were in midtown. They were certain the satirical poke at the elitist ad agencies would enhance their stature and desirability.

Announcements were sent to every client they ever served. Dave and Elisa followed up with calls to each of them to get them back in the fold.

Less than half the clients stayed on. Most of them had been Robbie's accounts. Despite the lower overhead of the new agency, profit was a challenge with their lower volume of business.

Dave began making sales calls in northern New Jersey and had some early success. The agency's creative portfolio was an excellent pitch tool. He had more difficulty in New York, as the barrier proved to be more psychological than geographic. This was caused by potential clients feeling insecure working with an agency in the suburbs.

Their remaining clients required a disproportionate volume of project business. While it was more profitable than advertising, it required a larger staff, was more sporadic and created downtime.

Elisa managed this workload by using a group of freelancers, rather than building a large team. Initially, she and Lainey managed the in-house operation while Dave divided his time between creative direction and sales.

At their next Friday date night, Dave caught Elisa by surprise by saying, "I'm sure you're not happy living in sin, so maybe we should get married?"

With a cynical look, she said, "You call that a proposal? We should get married because the church frowns on our living arrangement? My, you are a hopeless romantic, aren't you?"

Stammering, he said, "I guess I could have handled that a little better. But I don't have any experience doing this kind of thing. I don't even know how to date, much less propose marriage. I want to spend the rest of my life with you, with or without a certificate. And I would like to put a ring on your finger."

"Well, get the ring and then ask me."

Her opening was too good to let pass. "Why, does size matter?"

"Well, I overlooked it in your other category." By then the two of them were laughing uncontrollably and the other diners were all looking around to see what they were missing.

CHAPTER 72

Feeling at Home

AT LAINEY'S SUGGESTION, Dave and Elisa looked for an apartment in Ridgewood. It was a high-income village with huge mansions and a walkable downtown boasting upscale restaurants and shopping. There was also a commuter rail line that originated in Hoboken with a station in Ridgewood. The PATH line connected the Hoboken station with midtown New York City.

They found a large two-bedroom unit in a garden apartment complex on Ridgewood Avenue, convenient for their commute to work in Paramus. The real estate agent who rented the apartment was Sam Rayburn, an acquaintance of Lainey. He and his father owned the complex, as well as several others in the area. Knowing they were new to the area and being in the same age bracket, Sam befriended them and made recommendations for social activities.

Dave bought a car, giving them transportation flexibility, as bus service was limited in the county. He taught Elisa how to drive and she quickly got her license.

They continued their Friday night dates exploring the town's restaurants, learning that most restaurants in New Jersey were BYOB due to the limited number of on-premises liquor consumption licenses. The restaurants offered their patrons the opportunity to bring in their own alcoholic beverages, providing glasses and set-ups.

On one of their early dates, Elisa toasted their success at finding an excellent location for the business and their beautiful apartment with a garden and outdoor patio. In the ten years since leaving Bergen County, she saw that it had grown substantially with much more retail activity and energy.

She said, "Dave, I feel really good about being here. And you know how reluctant I was about moving back to New Jersey."

"We can succeed anywhere, and it's much safer here. Having lived in the mountains, I'll take all this foliage over the concrete canyons any day."

"Then we must explore the parks in the county. I also want to see the Delaware River and check out the area alongside Pennsylvania." Dave agreed, and on the weekends, they took excursions throughout the northern part of the state.

Their first drive was taking the Palisade Interstate Parkway from Fort Lee to the Bear Mountain Bridge. They had lunch at the Bear Mountain Inn and drove home through Harriman State Park.

They were both impressed with the beautiful cliffs along the Hudson River and the breathtaking mountains in the park, all so close to New York City. The excursion had Dave longing to again live in a wooded area.

In a hardware store on a Saturday morning, Dave encountered Sam Rayburn. As they chatted, Dave asked, "Are there any wooded building lots left in Bergen County? I would love to build a house on one."

"Oh sure. There's still plenty of land left for development here. If you'd like, I'll put together a package of lots for you to look at."

"Sure, but there's no hurry. I lived in the Adirondacks and would like to have a place that is secluded."

※　※　※

Dave surprised Elisa with a beautiful engagement ring he bought at a jewelry store in Ridgewood. The jeweler was a friend of Sam's and

Dave got an excellent discount. He presented it to her at a small restaurant in town that they frequented on their Friday Night dates. He had dropped off a bottle of champagne the night before and told the owner of his plan.

After they were seated at a table near the back, the waiter brought out a small charcuterie tray and said, "Compliments of the owner."

Sitting on top of the tray was a radicchio leaf, and on the leaf sat a ring box. Elisa looked at the box and then up at Dave. Smiling, he took her hand and offered her the ring, saying, "Will you marry this toothless, barefoot mountain hick who still can't afford a banjo?"

Thrilled, she laughed at his reference. With tears streaming down her face, she said, "Yes, I will."

The owner walked up to them carrying a tray with two glasses of champagne and the bottle, and announced to all, "Ladies and gentlemen, may I present the future Mr. and Mrs. Dave Powers."

All the patrons applauded.

CHAPTER 73

Potential Affiliation

ALTHOUGH SALES continued to grow, the agency struggled to make money. Their employees were still not being efficiently utilized. They had to keep a full staff as their clients expected the entire range of agency services. Dave was convinced a couple of media accounts generating magazine, radio, and TV commissions would smooth out the cash flow.

One of the freelancers told Dave about a small two-man agency with a few large media accounts that was looking to merge with an agency that had full design and production capabilities. Recognizing the potential fit, Dave contacted the agency and set up a meeting at his office.

Steve Kaufman and Marvin Edelstein sat in the conference room with Dave and Elisa to explore a potential merger. Kaufman described their client base, which was a small handful of media-driven accounts in the food industry plus their largest client, by far—a technology firm.

With technology emerging, this client was preparing to launch a major campaign requiring a plethora of services. The client was insisting the agency offer more in-house services than the two men could provide. A merger with a firm like Image Concepts could fulfill that requirement.

Edelstein also shared his vision of using mergers with other small

242 | ON THE BRINK

agencies to build a large full-service advertising and public relations agency in New Jersey. Dave found the concept intriguing, although Elisa remained much more cautious.

Dave described their capabilities and Elisa presented their portfolio, including the TV commercials they produced while at DBB. The two visitors were impressed and as the meeting broke up, they agreed to reconvene in a week.

After they left, Elisa went into Dave's office and said, "You seem pretty enthusiastic about this deal. Personally, I have some strong reservations."

"But they appear to be a perfect fit with the type of clients they have. The media income balances our production capabilities."

With her hands on his desk, she leaned over and said, "First of all, Kaufman is a creative director. You and I both fill that role. Do we need another one? And Edelstein gives me the creeps. My intuition is yelling in my ear with a bullhorn."

Bothered by her negativity, Dave said, "Let's meet with them again and see where it goes. We won't commit."

Walking back to her office, Elisa thought, *This just doesn't feel right.*

CHAPTER 74

Taking Root

Sᴀᴍ ʀᴀʏʙᴜʀɴ called Dave and told him he found a special lot that Dave had to see, but it wouldn't stay on the market for long. They met at lunchtime that day, and Sam took him to Ramsey, a small town a few miles further north from Ridgewood. They parked across the street from a pond and Sam pointed out the area on their side of the street as the lot. All Dave saw was a large, wooded area.

"Exactly where is the lot and how big is it?"

"The lot sits back about a thousand feet from the road. It's along this trail right here, which is an easement for a sewer main. The actual lot is five and a half acres. This easement will become your driveway back into the woods."

"You found a five-acre lot in Bergen County? It must cost a fortune. How much is it?"

"It's $75,000, but we'll negotiate. Let's walk back and take a look." The price shocked Dave.

They walked down the trail, which ran alongside a stream that was fed off the pond across the street. Sam was counting steps in his head and said, "It starts about here."

Dave looked back down the trail and could hardly see the street or the pond on the other side. The area around him was teeming with mature trees and underbrush. As he walked around, he saw deer tracks and pellets everywhere.

"Sam, I wasn't planning on building a house right now, or even buying a lot, but this is a once-in-a-lifetime opportunity. Contact the owner and tell him the property is sold."

"Wait a minute. First, I have to negotiate the price."

"Sam, you told me the average building lot in this part of Bergen County is one-quarter to one-half acre and goes for one hundred and fifty thousand. This is more than ten times that size for half the price. Why would I want to cut a deal? I want this lot. Period."

"But it's a flag lot that has an easement running through it, making it less valuable. Let me see what I can do. I promise I won't lose the deal."

Sam called back that night. "I got the lot for you. And you'll like the price."

"I liked the seventy-five thousand price."

"I offered thirty-seven thousand five hundred, and he said he wouldn't take less than fifty. We settled on forty-seven-five, and he'll take terms."

"Sam, you are amazing. I'll write a check. Now find me a builder."

"That's easy. My family is in the building business. Who do you think built the apartment complex you're in? I'll get our architect to work with you on a house plan."

The next day, Dave brought Elisa to walk the property. She had never seen him so excited. They trekked back to a small clearing in the center of the lot, and he said, "This is where we'll build our dream home."

"Oh, I don't know. It's in the middle of nowhere. What would I do if you were not home at night? There isn't another house within a mile of here."

"We'll put in an alarm system. Or get a big ugly dog. It will be safe for you. It's not New York City."

"I guess I'm used to having people around and this is so desolate. I'll have to get used to it. But I admit it is beautiful."

CHAPTER 75

Merger Offer

WHEN THE TWO PRINCIPALS of each agency got together for their second meeting, they discussed the terms of a potential merger. Edelstein suggested the four of them become equal partners in the new venture. He pointed out that the added billing from his agency would amortize the overhead and the merged agency would be more profitable.

Elisa was still apprehensive and wanted to take more time to determine the chemistry and working relationship that would evolve. She voiced strong trepidation, and they reluctantly concluded she was right.

Concerned that their client was under a time constraint, Edelstein suggested that he, Kaufman, and their office manager, Sandy, move into their offices and purchase services from them in lieu of rent. They all agreed to that arrangement, and the three of them moved in the following week.

After getting settled in their new offices, Dave and Kaufman discussed the overlap of responsibilities. Lainey would continue running the office, and their office manager Sandy would be the client contact for the K&E accounts and keep their books.

Within a week, however, Sandy began bickering with Lainey about procedures. She was territorial and became jealous of Lainey's role in running the support team. A couple of days later, she quit. Edelstein was upset at the development, concerned it would jeopardize their relationship with the K&E clients.

Kaufman continued to design the small volume of ads from their client base. Elisa's team produced the ads and Lainey placed them in the respective magazines. Their big technology client had yet to produce a single order, which troubled Elisa.

Less than a month later, Edelstein came into the office one morning excited about some news he heard at his country club the night before. A Clifton-based ad agency was up for sale. He had already called and set up a meeting with them.

Dave questioned him, "Shouldn't we complete our merger before we acquire another one?"

"Normally, I would agree. But when something like this becomes available, you have to move quickly."

The four of them visited the Pagano & Ryan agency in Clifton and met with the two owners. One was planning to retire while the other wanted to keep working. This was an ideal situation for maintaining client loyalty. They all agreed when Edelstein suggested that he should continue meeting and handle negotiations with the two owners.

Dave recognized that the current arrangement with K&E was cumbersome. The profit on the services provided was not covering the cost of their office space, making any acquisition difficult. At their Friday night dinner, Elisa brought it up. "Dave, completing these two deals at the same time is insane."

"I've been thinking the same thing."

"The acquisition is a good opportunity. I like Pagano. I don't like Edelstein and I don't want to be his partner."

Pouring more wine into their glasses, he hesitated to answer. "We can't do one without the other. Edelstein brought that deal, so we can't go around him. I also think your attitude towards him may be overblown."

Angry now, she said, "I'm sorry, but he grates on me and I have a bad premonition about him."

"At this point, we don't have much choice. We're losing money on the current arrangement we have with them, while they benefit from it. So, we have to merge. Edelstein will work out, I'm sure of it."

Elisa realized that he had made up his mind, so she backed off. *I hope I'm wrong, but I can sense danger coming.*

❋ ❋ ❋

Dave handled all the details of the merger. The new name would be Powers Orsini Kaufman & Edelstein, and their logo was POKE. Edelstein was not happy that his name was listed last, and Elisa was not happy with Edelstein.

With the deal done, Dave was convinced that the sporadic bleeding would stop, and the agency would quickly become profitable.

CHAPTER 76

A New Home

BEFORE DAVE met with the architect, he and Elisa took a drive to look at houses in the northern Bergen County area. He was intrigued with the historic homes from the Revolutionary War era. He pointed out a few that were homes of the original Dutch settlers.

Elisa agreed. "I love the Dutch-styled homes. They are so authentic for this part of the region."

"I was hoping you would like that style. I'll begin to sketch out how the whole house will look."

He came up with a Dutch Colonial home design that included a curved mansard roof with a stone veneer facade.

When he got to the inside layout, he told Elisa, "I think I'm going to go a little more contemporary on the inside."

"Will that work with a three-hundred-year-old exterior style?"

"I'm confident I can make it work."

Dave sketched an open-space ground floor that included a foyer, kitchen, dining area and living room, all under a ceiling that followed the curved shape of the roof. It would be twenty feet high at the apex with a large fireplace on the end wall. Three of the five doghouse dormers cut into the mansard roof would provide second-story light into the living area.

As Dave drew up the design sketches for the architect, an idea came to him for the wedding. When he told Elisa about it, she was delighted and asked Lainey to be her matron of honor. He asked Sam to be the best man. Sam suggested an attorney in Hackensack who was also a municipal judge to perform the ceremony.

※ ※ ※

The circular driveway in front of the house was nearly 1,500 feet long. Dave diverted the stream under the driveway in front of the house and used the water flow to build a small pond. As the site work was completed, the contractor poured the slab for the house. As soon as the concrete was set, Dave scheduled the wedding ceremony on the slab.

The municipal judge, Michael DeMarrais, performed the ceremony in front of the deer, fox, and other wildlife on the property. Sam's wife Rosie and Lainey's husband Dale joined the newlyweds at the Ramsey Country Club for an extravagant dinner. Overlooking the golf course, the dining room in the Abby consisted of a series of alcoves formed by stone arches taking visitors back to medieval Europe. The entire build was constructed from the same fieldstone, including the three-story tower at the entrance. It was a perfect setting to celebrate their marriage.

※ ※ ※

Three months after the wedding, they moved into their new home. The Dutch Colonial design with the weathered cedar shake siding fit perfectly within the mature trees and saplings that nestled the house. Falling in love with the natural setting, Elisa was thrilled with the outcome. Once they moved in, she used her design talent to decorate the interior.

A herd of about thirty deer traipsed through the yard about once a week, eating any flowers that were planted. The pond was visited by a pair of Canadian geese who delivered their goslings there every spring before traveling south, and a fox family became the local pets.

Both Dave and Elisa envisioned many years of happiness in their beautiful home.

CHAPTER 77

Forty Love

SAM RAYBURN called Dave at the office with an invitation. "Dave, next week there is a charity event in Fort Lee, and I want you and Elisa to attend as my guests. It will be a chance to meet some new people on a social basis, and maybe even find a new client."

"That's very generous of you. What are the details?"

"On Saturday morning, there's a tennis party at the Fort Lee Racquet Club that ties in with the US Open. Some lesser-known women tennis stars will be on hand to play with the guests. That evening there's a formal ball at the Alpine Country Club."

"What an impressive venue. I'll check with Elisa."

When Elisa got back to the office, Dave told her about the invitation and the potential networking opportunity. Although she was overjoyed, she said, "I don't have clothes for either the tennis party or the ball. We'll have to go shopping tonight."

After work, they went to Lord & Taylor and Elisa looked for a tennis outfit that would be appropriate for the event. She found one that was perfect, but it was expensive.

"This is far more than I would ever spend on a dress I expect to sweat in."

They then went to the formal wear department and looked for a gown. She had difficulty finding something that flattered her body, but the sales associate brought one out that made her look taller with its tight-fitting shape. Slits on the sides emphasized her shapely legs. Dave was amazed by how beautiful she looked in the gown.

On the way home, she complained to Dave that her chest looked even smaller the way the bodice was cut. She said, "Men like big boobs, and mine are too small. I wish they were bigger."

"That's just not true. You have beautiful breasts that are firm and perfectly shaped."

"You're saying that to make me feel good, but I know men salivate over big tits."

"Look, I don't have a lot of experience with boobs, but I've been in the company of two women with exceptionally large ones. And while they looked great standing at a bar, the clothes hid a lot of flaws. One woman in particular, Jackie, had really unattractive breasts. They were beyond unsightly. After seeing them, it made me appreciate smaller, nicely shaped breasts."

"Now I know you're lying."

On Saturday morning, they arrived at the racquet club and went into their respective dressing rooms to change. Elisa came out of the ladies' locker room and rushed up to Dave and said, "When you told me about big boobs the other night, I didn't believe you. But there's a woman in there, changing into a sports bra who has the biggest, ugliest breasts I've ever seen. I couldn't believe what they looked like."

Smiling, Dave said, "Someday, just maybe, you will accept that I am always honest with you."

Just then an attractive woman came out of the locker room, and when Dave looked up, he was shocked. "Hi Jackie, how have you been?" he said. "Meet my wife, Elisa."

The daggers from Elisa kept coming all morning and Dave just looked at her and shrugged.

At the banquet, they were seated with four other couples including Sam and his wife. One of the women worked for a mail-order house, and when she heard about their agency she invited Elisa to visit her office. They exchanged business cards.

CHAPTER 78

Agency Acquisition

EDELSTEIN CAME BACK to the office from a meeting with Pagano and Ryan and announced they had reached a deal to acquire their agency. POKE would pay them $200,000 upfront and an additional $200K at the end of each year for three years. Pagano would join POKE as a senior account executive at $100K per year and manage all their accounts after Ryan retired. Their agency's previous year's gross profit was $600,000.

Since Edelstein was the only partner that had any experience with ad agency mergers. The other three accepted the terms in good faith, although Elisa and Dave thought the price was too high. He decided to do some research and learned that recent sales of ad agencies averaged the equivalent of one year's gross profit of business retained.

Realizing that the terms were far too generous, and they grossly overpaid for the acquisition, he confronted Edelstein. "You just committed us to a bad deal. How can you justify it?"

"Look, Dave. You don't know anything about M and A. Pagano's largest client is about to double its size with the purchase of its largest competitor. It will increase their budget by 80 percent. That alone will make the deal far better and it will cost us nothing extra."

Dave sighed. "We'd better hope that happens, or we may be in deep shit."

With both the merger and the acquisition complete, Dave and the bookkeeper began to transfer all the accounts to one set of books. He was shocked at the salaries and expenses Kaufman and Edelstein were taking.

They each received $250,000 a year. They also had country club memberships paid by the company, multiple credit card accounts, plus extraordinary entertainment expenses. Fortunately, Pagano was drawing a salary closer to 100K, but it would still be a heavy drain in the short term.

Elisa and Dave both liked Joe Pagano and thought he would fit in well with the team. Over six feet tall and slightly stooped, with a balding head and dark circles around his brown eyes, he gave the appearance of a professor. But he was a savvy executive and smiled when he spoke with his deep authoritative voice.

Dave called a brief meeting with Kaufman and Edelstein and urged them to reduce their salaries and expenses until profits picked up. He pointed out that their clients' billing was down substantially from when they negotiated their deal. The technology client still had not provided its first order.

Both refused, saying they couldn't afford to reduce their income. They also pointed out that even with media accounts, there was an ebb and flow to their billing, and Edelstein countered that their big account was about to launch its huge campaign.

There was still the matter of the $200,000 due to Pagano and Ryan. Dave told his partners they each had to invest $50,000 for the down payment, and another $25,000 to maintain cash flow until the billing started to flow. They balked at this and finally agreed to pay the $50,000 and add the rest if needed.

Since they were equal partners, Dave increased his and Elisa's salaries to match theirs and began charging all their expenses to the company. Dave broached the idea to Elisa that they consider joining a country club. She balked, suggesting instead they take some golf lessons and start playing at public courses. They could always have the company cover those costs.

While the compensation increase was great to have, Dave was uncomfortable with the cash flow drain taking place. He discussed it with Elisa, and she reviewed the books. She was shocked at Edelstein's expenses on top of all their oversize salaries. It was all unsustainable unless sales increased immediately.

Then the opposite happened. Edelstein's big account sent a letter terminating their relationship with the agency. When the letter arrived, Dave immediately called a partnership meeting. As managing partner, Dave demanded they each invest the additional twenty-five K. He also said, "We all have to take a salary cut and reduce our expenses in half."

Edelstein answered, "There you go, jumping into panic mode again. We can handle this blip."

"Blip? This isn't a blip. They represented nearly seventy percent of your billing. It's a major blow to our solvency. I'm having the bookkeeper prepare a cash flow report to show you how precarious our situation is."

"I don't have to see any reports. I know we're going to be fine. We'll all cut back a little."

Elisa jumped into the fray. "Marvin, are you aware you spend more money on expenses than the other three of us combined?"

"Well, I'm the rainmaker, here. I spend it on entertainment to get new customers."

Incensed, she came back with, "Do you have prospects in Syracuse, where your son goes to college? Or Boston, where your daughter is in grad school?" Edelstein squirmed at that revelation, furious that Elisa had checked his expenses.

Infuriated to learn this, Kaufman spoke out. "Marvin, do your kids have company credit cards?"

"Yes, but they don't spend as much as your wife does with her card."

Dave ended the conversation with his directive. "From now on, no expenses will be paid unless absolutely necessary. This includes your wives and kids, and your country clubs. Pay them out of your own pocket. And if business doesn't pick up quickly, I'm cutting all our salaries. By a lot!"

CHAPTER 79

Trouble in Paradise

THE DAY AFTER the blowout meeting, Kaufman went to the bookkeeper and asked to look at the credit card records, plus the accounts payable and receivable. After reviewing everything, he realized that Dave was right about the cash flow. They were in serious trouble. His review also proved Elisa's comment about Edelstein's over-the-top expenses.

He went out to lunch the next day with Edelstein and unloaded on him. "When we started making money, we raised our salaries accordingly, and we had an unspoken agreement to charge our country clubs and reasonable personal expenses to the company."

"And that's what I've been doing."

"Bullshit! Your kid must be supporting a brewery up in Syracuse. Your daughter is right behind him with her spending, not to mention your wife's spa treatments and department store charges. And you had the balls to comment on my wife's charges?"

"Oh, well, maybe it's getting a little out of hand."

"Out of hand? They're charging twenty-five to fifty thousand a year, plus what you spend. You haven't brought in a new account in over two years. And we just lost our anchor client."

"I'm working on some new business. We'll see some activity in the next month."

"Well, if we don't, I'm going to make you pay back some of the excessive charges your family made to the company."

❄ ❄ ❄

Pagano ended the call with his client by slamming the phone receiver down. He walked into Dave's office and told him the news. His hardware client's purchase of its competitor fell through at the last minute.

This stunned Dave. "If you can't replace that potential business, we're going to have to renegotiate our deal. There isn't enough profit to support the money we're paying you."

"Dave, the contract is solid, and we're not changing the terms."

"Look, neither one of us wants a confrontation. You've been in the business a long time. Go find another client. Right now, the agency can't handle these hits to its billing."

In the next two months, the mood at the agency went from euphoric to depressing. Dave recognized that an ad agency cannot perform without enthusiasm and a winning culture. He called an all-employee meeting the following day at lunchtime and had Lainey order pizzas and soft drinks.

While everyone was wolfing down slices of pizza, he made his speech.

"This ad agency has enjoyed tremendous growth since Elisa and I reestablished it here a few years ago. And everyone in this room has contributed to that success. More recently, we've hit a few major challenges that are impacting our financial health.

"Business that we anticipated and planned for has fallen through. And now our overhead is choking our cash flow. And if we don't add some new clients, we're going to be forced to take some painful steps."

One of the designers asked, "Will you have to lay people off?"

"Not at the moment. I'm trying to avoid layoffs or salary cuts, but it all comes down to increasing sales. While Marvin is our new business executive, selling is now everybody's job. I want each of you to take a look at your family, friends, and neighbors. If any of them has a business or works for a mid-size company, ask them if they would consider a presentation from one of the most creative ad agencies in New Jersey."

The bookkeeper commented, "I wouldn't know what to say. I can't even describe what we do."

"I get that. Here's how we'll do this. If you think you have a prospect, we'll coach you on what to say. And if there's even a little interest, one of the partners will follow up. If a lead from anyone on the staff becomes an account, that person will get a bonus check."

A buzz followed Dave's comments, and the energy immediately picked up at the prospect of positive activity.

CHAPTER 80

A Break in the Action

A MONTH AFTER Dave's directive to the staff, neither Edelstein nor Pagano had brought in a new account. The other staff's referrals resulted in a few brochure projects, but nothing of any substance. Nevertheless, despite the size of the orders, the agency provided small bonuses for these new projects.

Calling the partners into his office, Dave told them that they each had to invest another $25,000 into the company to keep it solvent.

Edelstein cried that he couldn't afford it. "I have huge college tuition bills."

This angered Kaufman. "No, Marvin. The three of us will put up another twenty-five thousand, but you're writing a check for fifty thousand to make up for some of the money your family keeps charging to the agency." Edelstein sat there, fuming, but had no comeback.

The cash infusion kept the agency's payables current for another few months, but there was still no new business added to the client list. Then Elisa got a call from a friend in New York City who told her about a client looking for an agency.

She and Dave visited the account to make a pitch. The company, Bucolic Farms, produced a line of bottled salad dressings that they distributed in supermarkets. The owner became infatuated with Elisa and her ideas about marketing the line. They returned to the office with the agency's first new client since the merger.

Everyone was ecstatic over the account, and it lifted the cloud of gloom that had been hanging over the agency. Edelstein, however, was miffed that he wasn't asked to participate in the pitch. He cited all his experience with their other food accounts. Dave and Elisa ignored him.

While Kaufman was relieved over the win, he was troubled that Edelstein still had not brought in a new client. He went into his office and told him how he felt. This led to an argument with Kaufman threatening further income cuts and storming out.

At their Friday night dinner date, Dave suggested to Elisa they take a vacation. They hadn't taken a day off since opening the agency in New Jersey, often working on weekends. She agreed that it was important for them to recharge their batteries.

On Monday, Dave told Kaufman and Edelstein about their planned one-week trip to the Adirondacks, and he told them both to take a vacation. "We all need to take a break and regroup."

Edelstein said, "That's a good idea. We were thinking of visiting my son at school. Maybe we'll extend it and drive down through the Finger Lakes."

"The stress is affecting us all," Kaufman added. "I wasn't planning anything, but a getaway with my wife will benefit us both. She's been so busy with her real estate sales that she and her boss are both burned out."

Dave said, "Then it's agreed. We'll each take time off a couple of weeks apart."

Edelstein and his wife left for Syracuse two weeks later, and after a month the Kaufmanns flew to Chicago with her boss and his wife for a junket to the Windy City.

CHAPTER 81

Trouble at Home

THE WEEK BEFORE Dave and Elisa were scheduled to leave for Indian Lake, she came into the office early on a Saturday morning to wrap up a small project. She was surprised to find Kaufman sitting at his desk unfocused, his face blotchy and eyes bloodshot.

"Steve, why are you here?" she asked. "I thought you were in Chicago. What's wrong?"

Without trying to hide his discomfort, he said, "My wife left me."

"What! You were on vacation. Did something happen?"

"She's been having an affair with her boss for years. I was shocked to find out. They told us one night when the four of us were at a bar in Chicago."

"Oh, how awful."

"His wife left the bar, went to her room, packed, and took a cab to the airport. I think she suspected something for a long time. I had no idea."

"What are you going to do?"

"We talked all night, but it made no difference. Our marriage went flat years ago. She said she didn't want to hurt me, but she couldn't continue like this. We cut the trip short and she moved out as soon as we got home. She and her boss have been quietly sharing an apartment for over a year."

Saddened by the news, she asked, "What are you going to do? Do you have any plans?"

"We're going to sell the house and I'm going to move to New Jersey to be closer to the office."

"Let me know how we can help you. Do you want to come over for dinner tonight?"

"Thank you, but no. I'm going to Fort Lee and look for an apartment. Then I'm meeting some friends for a late dinner."

After Kaufman left, Elisa completed her project and drove home. She wondered how he was going to function under these circumstances. *The distraction will stifle his creativity.*

Kaufman quickly found an apartment on the Palisades in Fort Lee and took a few days off work to move in. Once he was settled, he sat on his balcony overlooking New York City, sipped brandy, and unwound from the stress of a loveless marriage and the final separation. He was now ready to take on the challenges of work and deal with his longtime business partner.

CHAPTER 82

Rest and Relaxation

WITH THE CAR PACKED, Dave and Elisa left for Indian Lake early on a Saturday morning. They checked into the Lone Birch Inn, unpacked, and went uptown to pick up LeRoy. The three of them drove down the mountain, past the whitewater stretch of the Hudson River to the Gore Mountain Inn in North Creek. They enjoyed dinner at the beautiful rustic lodge.

Elisa was fascinated by LeRoy's energy and active mind. She knew he was in his late seventies, but he moved and talked like he was forty. He told them about the many ways the town was changing. Most of the young people were still moving away after college, but a lot more people were coming up from the cities and building vacation homes there.

Dave spoke to him about cleaning up his property and selling it. LeRoy agreed that it was an attractive site for a home with its beautiful river view. He said he would get a couple of the younger men to truck the debris to the town dump and clean up the site. Once complete, he could put it up for sale.

Over the next few days, Dave took Elisa around to see the splendor the wilderness area had to offer. First, he took her to his property, and she saw the burned-out remains of his house and studio. She became choked up seeing the destruction of the once-beautiful site.

They then drove past the shores of Indian Lake and climbed

Snowy Mountain. Exhausted after the hike, they drove back to the motel, showered, and went to dinner. On Monday, Dave took her on the trail to the top of Chimney Mountain and showed her the cave where his father lost his life. Later in the afternoon, they visited Marty's Tavern and saw a few of the friends Dave had made in town. Ted Spring was there, and Dave introduced him to Elisa. He told them he was still building the guide boats and had three people working for him.

As the evening wound down, Elisa said, "You must have mixed emotions about returning here. I see the beauty that draws you to this place, but I also feel the sadness connected with your time here." Dave looked at her lovingly and wrapped his arms around her.

The next morning, they left the Lone Birch, which Dave referred to as the Love Bitch. She said, "That inference doesn't refer to me, does it?"

"Only if you feel a connection." And then he winced from the punch in the ribs.

Driving down the mountain, Dave turned into the long drive to the Sutrinas vacation home. No one was at the house, but Dave drove around to show her the enormous tract of untamed vistas.

After spending a few days in Lake George, they drove back to Ramsey. Elisa was overwhelmed by the beauty of the mountains, rivers, and lakes. *It was vast and unspoiled just as Dave described. I see how both he and Robbie were so attracted to it.* She now understood why Dave was so thrilled about building their home on the five-acre wooded lot, 1,500 feet from the street in Ramsey.

CHAPTER 83

The Confrontation

WHILE ELISA AND DAVE were enjoying their much-needed vacation, the agency was suffering further setbacks. Pagano's second-largest client, a manufacturer of consumer electronic components, was sold to a much larger company. The entire product line was being rolled into the parent company's brand, resulting in the agency losing the account.

A large batch of contaminated product was distributed by Bucolic Farms, forcing them to announce a recall of their products from all the supermarkets. It would be months before they could recover, if at all.

As the bad news rolled in, Edelstein sat in his office immobilized with fear by the fiscal challenges facing the agency. He was unable to make sales calls or deal with the situation. Kaufman, seeing his partner's catatonic state, became incensed and called him into the conference room.

They argued for half an hour and in the end Edelstein blamed Kaufman for his failure to sell new accounts.

That did it for Kaufmann. "We're finished. I'm finally seeing the picture clearly. We're breaking up this agency and we're each going our separate ways. I'll put together a plan. As soon as Dave and Elisa get back, we'll set it in motion. In the meantime, you can pack up your shit, because you're done."

"Listen to yourself. Stop panicking. We're going to be just fine. I'll be bringing in new business any day."

"That's good. If you get this phantom account, keep it, because you'll need it to support yourself. We're broke. We can't make Pagano's payment, and we're going to have trouble making payroll. It's over, Marvin. Get out now and support yourself."

Kaufman got up and went back to his office. Devasted by Kaufman's ultimatum, Edelstein sat there immobilized, thinking, *How could the partner I supported for ten years, throw me under the bus?*

CHAPTER 84

An Ugly Divorce

ON SUNDAY NIGHT after they returned home, Dave got a call from Kaufman about his decision and his conversation with Edelstein. After the call, he sat down with Elisa and shared the news.

"Actually, I'm relieved," he told her. "I've always been good about handling stress, but Edelstein has been getting to me. Let's both think about it tonight, and tomorrow we'll ride in together and talk about a strategy."

"I hate to rub it in, but I knew from the first time I met him he'd be disruptive. Women have this gene that doesn't exist in men and we can tell the difference between real men and pretenders. Marvin had a flashing light over his head."

"You were right. I should have listened to you and not been so impulsive."

"Running this business has stopped being fun. How are we financially?"

"There's only a little money left in the Bahamas account, probably enough to carry us for a while, but that's it. Worst case, we sell this house."

"We're not selling this house. I know now how important it is to you."

In the car the next morning, Dave told Elisa his concept for going forward. "I'm getting burned out building and rebuilding our ad agency just for some outside force to destroy it. Why do we have to staff up and run a full-service agency?"

"No client would consider doing business with us if we didn't offer a full range of agency services. The bureaucratic clients feel too insecure otherwise."

"I don't agree. The current economy is pointing in a different direction. We brand our shop as an efficient operation offering professional-level service with trend-setting creativity at dramatically reduced costs through low overhead. It will sell."

"Again, you're battling their anxiety. They are buying peace of mind, not creativity."

"Not all of them. Especially not the entrepreneurial companies, and the savvy marketing VPs at the larger firms. Those are the clients I want, not the guys who hide under their desks afraid of failure."

"Dave, you are right, but you're also reducing your prospect market by taking the weaklings out of the equation."

"I've never been comfortable with the clients who can't make a decision. I think there's plenty of savvy clients left if we stay small, maybe just the two of us. In that way, we can be profitable without a lot of accounts. Let's go meet with Kaufman and see what he has to say."

When they arrived, they walked into the conference room where Edelstein and Kaufman were seated. Edelstein looked like he hadn't slept all weekend. Kaufman, on the other hand, looked fresh and more relaxed than ever. He led the meeting.

"Here's how the salvage operation is going to go. Pagano will forgo the balance of payments owed to him. He and I are taking over the existing agency, including the payables, receivables, and the debt to Ryan. The new name will be Kaufman and Pagano. We will also take all the advertising clients. Marvin is leaving immediately and going out on his own."

"Dave and Elisa will revert back to their original agency and keep all the collateral and promotion accounts. Elisa will handle all the typesetting and mechanical production for the Kaufman & Pagano clients at current rates."

"There is no negotiating these terms. If we don't agree, we file bankruptcy immediately. Any questions?"

When everyone nodded consent, he continued with the remaining details of the plan.

"The staff will be terminated on Friday with a small severance check. I will meet with them right after we're done. If anyone has questions, I'll be in my office the rest of the day. Good luck to us all."

CHAPTER 85

Planning Ahead

ELISA FOLLOWED Dave into his office and asked, "So, what do you think?"

"I think it's the best scenario under the circumstances. We get to keep our project accounts, which the two of us can handle on our own. I'll do the creative, and you can do all the production."

"What about all the money and sweat we put into the agency. I feel like it all got flushed down the toilet."

"Yes, it did. And it's the second time it happened to us. That's what I was talking about this morning. I don't want to go through that again."

Exhaling her frustration, Elisa said, "I feel like we wasted all those years and have nothing to show for it."

"We failed at building a substantive, profitable agency, but we did support ourselves with an upper middle-class lifestyle. Just look at the house we built. And we still have a book of business that has value. If we stay small, we can continue to live very comfortably. I told you I'm not looking to be a millionaire. It's not worth the stress."

Shortly before noon, Kaufman called the entire staff into the conference room. They all stood around knowing what was coming. He told them about the agency breakup and their termination. Handing out the severance checks, he wished them all good luck.

After the brief meeting, Lainey walked into Elisa's office and sat down. "I guess I've been dumped again. I think I'm going to retire this time. Dale has been talking about moving to the Carolinas."

"Don't start packing yet. David and I are working on something. I'll share it with you as soon as it's solid."

Dave wrote a script outline to describe their new venture and discussed it with Elisa. He decided to revive their original name, Image Concepts, and promoted it as an efficient, low-overhead restructure of their agency. Agreeing to the talking points, they each got on the phone and called the clients with their new pitch.

It was an easy sell. The clients were familiar with the quality of their work and welcomed a lower rate structure. Elisa ran into Dave's office, "Every client I spoke to said yes."

"I'm getting the same response. It's because our clients know us. It will be more difficult when we pitch new accounts, but here's what we'll do. Going forward, we'll ask our clients to write a recommendation letter describing their experience with us. And we'll use those letters to sell new accounts on our low-overhead model."

They then sat and estimated their new overhead and the average monthly billing for each of the retained clients. The projected profit margins were impressive.

"I'm comfortable with the numbers," Elisa said, "and I'm confident we can grow it from this base. Let's do it!"

She then called Lainey. "You'd better tell Dale to put the Carolinas on hold for a few more years."

PART V

Testing a New Concept

CHAPTER 86

Deja Vu with a Twist

Resuming the operation under its previous name, Image Concepts was up and running in a week at its new 500-square-feet location on Route 17. It was only three miles from their previous location, in a building off the highway at a much lower rent rate. Dave had arranged to take their furniture from the agency, and Lainey joined them as soon as the furniture arrived. Within the first few months, the fledgling three-employee shop showed promise. With the benefit of its low overhead, the existing clients were delighted to reap the savings.

Edelstein called in the late afternoon on a Friday and asked Dave if he and Elisa would consider a partnership with him. He claimed he had more new business than he could handle alone.

Dave told him, "Marvin, we're experiencing a similar issue with our new model and have no interest in bringing anyone on board." He then added, "Good luck." Without waiting for a reply, he hung up and smiled.

❀ ❀ ❀

One morning, Elisa's former Hackensack neighbor Joan Romano walked in and surprised Elisa. They had been friends going back to when they were both living at home. After the hugs and kisses, she told Elisa she had left MetLife's health insurance group and was taking a job with a health care consulting firm.

When Elisa explained what the agency did, Joan perked up. "A close friend of mine is handling marketing for one of the divisions at MetLife. That group is introducing a new healthcare model, and they need lots of brochures to promote the coverage."

"That's exactly what we do. Can you make an introduction?"

Joan got on the phone and called her contact, introducing Elisa to her. Elisa explained their agency's services and how their new model worked. The marketing manager was intrigued and invited her to visit their office and make a presentation.

Elisa went into the city and presented their portfolio to the marketing team. Impressed with the level of creativity, they were awarded the huge project, which was the largest program they had done since moving to New Jersey. Valued at over $200,000, Elisa had to call in a couple of freelancers to expedite the volume of material needed.

A reporter from *Adweek* called Elisa and asked about their new agency concept. He had heard from a client who was using them and he was curious about its acceptance. She explained the virtual ad agency model and how they were successful from day one. Surprised by the results, he wrote a brief article in his publication.

This led to a call from the president of the National Advertising Federation who was sponsoring a forum on alternate income sources and models for the future of advertising agencies. He invited them to speak at the conference.

They accepted and went to the event where Dave spoke about how they structured their agency as a cost-saving solution to escalating advertising expenses. The concept was well received by client companies looking to get a higher return on their marketing investment.

The agency got dozens of calls following the event, but Dave and

Elisa were selective about which clients to pursue. Some were much too big for their operation, while others appeared to be tire kickers looking to cut costs without regard to performance.

Over the next two years, Image Concepts maintained a gradual growth in profitability. Their model, using outside consultants and freelancers, worked well. They were very comfortable financially, but the huge profits never materialized.

During a Friday night date, they discussed their situation and compared it to everything they had experienced in the past.

"We could make as much at a New York agency producing exciting campaigns, but it's not worth all that grief again," Elisa said.

"It was just as exciting building a successful agency from scratch," Dave said, "but the devastating challenges outside our control are not something I ever want to face again."

Elisa sipped her wine. "We're very comfortable and have no worries. Plus, there's the equity in the house if money ever becomes a problem."

Dave thought for a moment. "The only issue I see is we're not building a retirement fund. I don't know if this virtual agency has any virtual value if we opt to sell it."

"We have time to work on that in the future. Right now I feel safe and happy, and that's worth more than any amount of money we can earn."

Raising his glass and clinking his wife's, Dave added, "Elisa, we're living the dream. We make enough to live well and love what we do. We have plenty of leisure time, and it truly is stress-free."

CHAPTER 87

Shocking Discovery

DURING HER ANNUAL health checkup, Elisa's doctor recommended a mammogram. Elisa questioned it, saying, "I'm still in my thirties. Why now?"

"It's a precaution. There's nothing to indicate you have an issue, but research is pointing to getting these tests at an earlier age. Breast cancer is less prevalent among younger women, but far deadlier."

Accepting his advice, she made an appointment for a mammogram. The results indicated a small lump in her left breast. Surgery was scheduled to remove the lump and biopsy it. Elisa was nervous as the surgery date approached, but Dave kept calming her down.

"There is nothing wrong with you. It's precautionary, and I'm certain it's benign." *There's no way she has cancer. We're both healthy and strong.*

Dave accompanied Elisa to the hospital for the procedure and alternately sat and paced in the lobby awaiting a report from the surgeon. Still in his scrubs, the doctor came directly from the OR and shared his findings.

The surgeon explained the pea-size tumor seen in the X-ray was now the size of an acorn.

"I can see it's malignant even without taking a biopsy, and it has already started to spread within the breast. This type of cancer is extremely aggressive, and I'm concerned it may have already started to spread to other parts of her body."

Stunned, Dave stood there immobilized and finally struggled to ask, "Is she going to be okay?"

"I can't answer that right now. I'm rushing the biopsy and we'll schedule a meeting with her oncologist to determine her prognosis. Let's wait and get all the facts before anyone panics."

As the surgeon walked back into the OR, Dave slumped back in his chair, feeling like he was going to pass out. *Am I going to lose my Elisa? Our best years are still in front of us.*

Dave waited in the recovery room for his wife to awaken from the anesthesia. He was crushed by the news and didn't know what to tell her when she awoke.

Sitting in the darkened room, he got choked up and wanted to get in bed and hold her. The air in the room was stifling and all the hospital odors were making him lightheaded. He kept asking himself, *Why does everyone close to me get taken away?*

A nurse came into the room to check on Elisa, and seeing Dave sitting there, she asked if she could get him anything? He declined.

When Elisa came to, she was still groggy. Seeing Dave's state, she said, "Oh, no. It's bad, isn't it?"

He jumped up and reached across the bed to hold her, trying to pull himself together.

He blurted out, "Oh, Elisa. It's a really aggressive type of breast cancer. It may have already spread."

Just then, the surgeon came in and, hearing Dave's explanation, stopped him. He corrected Dave, explaining his early prognosis and that they should wait until the biopsy results are in and they had met with the oncologist.

"We're going to do everything we can, but please don't jump to conclusions. I'm already in consultation with the oncologist, and we'll know more when we get the results of the biopsy. You'll almost certainly need a mastectomy and chemo."

After the surgeon left, the nurse came back in to check Elisa's vitals and prepare her for release. Both Dave and Elisa continued to hold hands both in the hospital and all the way home.

When they arrived, he put her in bed and climbed in beside her. They held each other until they both fell asleep.

CHAPTER 88

Good as New

THE BIOPSY CAME BACK from the lab and, with the scheduled MRI, confirmed the surgeon's original prognosis. This was an aggressive strain. Elisa's oncologist reviewed the data and recommended a double mastectomy, followed by a chemo cocktail taken intravenously for six months. The strong doses would debilitate her for two days after each treatment, and then she would be able to perform normally. Hopefully, this drastic combination would extend her life expectancy.

The treatments began and Elisa was able to manage them without too much difficulty. But during that time, they both lived with the trepidation that it was all a discomforting waste of time.

After the second MRI, Dave and Elisa met with the oncologist at his office. He had all the images up on a screen and he showed her the improvement from the chemo.

He said, "I am far more encouraged by the results than I was before we started. Back then I doubted we could turn this around."

Dave said, "Does this mean she'll be okay?"

"I can't answer that, but now I feel she has at least a chance to live a near-normal life."

Elisa smiled and said, "I can't ask for more than that."

The oncologist then explained the next steps. This would include breast reconstruction and ongoing medication for at least five years.

When they got home, Elisa cried into Dave's chest, both from relief as well as the upcoming disfiguration and the unknown. Between sobs, she said, "I'm going to lose my breasts and be left with scars on my chest. How awful. But it will give me a chance to survive."

"Oh, Elisa. You'll get reconstruction and you will look fine."

"But it's scary. After the prognosis, I read that women who have mastectomies experience an extraordinary rate of divorce. Men have trouble accepting the reality of implants."

"You're talking about materialistic men. You know me better. I married you for who you are. I love who you are." Smiling, he added, "I always liked your tiny boobs, and I will love your fake boobs, too."

"I think it's going to be a difficult adjustment to have these plastic balloons in my chest."

With a smirk, he said, "That may be true, but now's your chance to have the size you always wanted. You are going for the double Ds, aren't you?

His comment made her smile as well.

CHAPTER 89

Consulting Gig

Eᴌɪsᴀ's ʀᴇᴄᴏɴsᴛʀᴜᴄᴛɪᴏɴ went well, and she was declared free of cancer. However, she was now saddled with a barrage of new medications to be taken on a daily basis, probably for the rest of her life.

Joan Romano called for an update on her recovery and was delighted to hear she had returned to her normal activity level. She told Elisa she was consulting for a health insurer in Rhode Island at a huge monthly fee. She said, "The company is called RIHIP, Rhode Island Health Insurance Partners. It lost its monopoly on the health care market there but still acts like it owns the state. They lost twenty-five million this year and are projecting a similar loss next year."

"How can they afford to pay you?"

"They brought in our entire team to restore the company to profitability. The competition is eating their lunch and they need to turn it around. I'll have Dave up here in no time to do some projects."

"It sounds exciting. I'm sure Dave would enjoy working with you."

When Elisa told Dave about her conversation with Joan, he said, "Rhode Island is a three-hour drive from here. It will be difficult to service them going up and back in one day."

"First, let's see if she comes through. She also couldn't believe how quickly I recovered."

"I'm amazed at that myself. In fact, I've been thinking about taking you on vacation. We haven't been away since starting this new agency. There's a tennis and golf camp in Killington, Vermont. Would you be up for a five-day trip there over a long weekend?"

"Great idea. My doctor said I can resume all my regular activities. Let's book it."

The drive to Killington was beautiful, reminiscent of their trip to the Adirondacks. The camp was at the base of the ski area, and it used ski lodges for housing. They spent two days of intense golf instruction and one day on the tennis courts. In the evenings they enjoyed dinner at the rustic restaurants including Casey's Caboose and the Wobbly Barn.

They were exhausted driving home, but were also exhilarated by the experience. After all the lessons, Elisa wanted to join a country club and play more golf. The exposure to the views of the ski area intrigued them both and they talked about returning in the winter to learn to ski.

Dave said, "Look, we don't have to worry about money, so let's spend more time on recreational activities. After your scare, I don't want to miss out on any fun we can do together."

CHAPTER 90

Investigative Overview

Dave LEFT THE HOUSE at 5:30 a.m. and drove to Providence, Rhode Island to meet Joan for a nine o'clock meeting. He allowed a half-hour cushion for traffic and arrived at 8:45. He was ushered into a small conference room where Joan introduced him to one of the product marketing managers and the director of sales.

The team described the company's plight, having gone from 85 percent market share to 49 percent in only three years. In the fiscal year just ended, the firm lost $26 million with no letup in sight. Joan's consulting group was reorganizing the sales department and introducing a broker model to increase sales.

Dave's assignment was to do a needs analysis and a competitive intelligence report on the marketing campaigns of the three new competitors that had infiltrated the Rhode Island marketplace. After the meeting, Joan took Dave to the Capital Grill for lunch.

"This company got too comfortable being a monopoly," she said. "For years they were fat, dumb, and happy. Now everyone is scared to death that their cushy, lifetime jobs may be terminated."

He commented, "I noticed. You could see the puddles of sweat in the meetings."

"I want you to come back up here and spend up to a week studying the other insurers' advertising. Interview anyone in the company you choose. I can set up meetings with some of our clients, our outside brokers, and state legislators if you want."

"Yes, I'd like to talk to lots of people on the ground. Make a list of contacts that you suggest and assign someone to me from your department to be my liaison. I'll be back up next week."

On the way home, Dave thought about the potential of this account. The distance troubled him, but it was an exciting and unique project. *If I'm going to take on this client, I'm going to have to raise my fees, given the amount of travel time.*

CHAPTER 91

Market Research

F OR THE NEXT WEEK, Dave played detective as he interviewed scores of people inside the company and around the state. He spent his evenings watching TV and making notes about the competition's advertising.

On Thursday, he drove up to Boston to meet the principals of RIHIP's advertising agency. He was impressed with their portfolio but horrified by the advertising they created for the insurer.

"Why the disparity in your creative product?"

The agency partner handling the account was candid. "It's the responsibility of RIHIP's VP of Marketing, who has no understanding of advertising or marketing. He's a sales guy and not very good at that. He's convinced the ads should look subdued and institutional, like banking ads. He wants to project security and longevity."

"Well, the competition's ads have much more energy."

"We're aware of that. But our day-to-day contact is the AVP of Marketing. He also has no clue about the process and just wants to maintain the status quo."

Dave was taken aback. "So, the advertising budget is wasted on commercials that get no results."

❉ ❉ ❉

On Friday afternoon, Dave returned to Ramsey and met Elisa at Look See Restaurant for dinner. As they shared a bottle of wine and orders of Peking Duck, he described his amazing week to her. "The biggest lesson I learned is that Rhode Island is a foreign country. It doesn't function like any part of America."

"How could you say that? How different can it be?"

"It would take me a week to explain it all. I might even write a book about it someday. The employees are friendly, but suspicious of outsiders. They're all lifers, hired out of college or high school. They're terrified of losing their jobs. No one takes the initiative to make even minor changes. And no one can make a decision. Oh, and they're all related."

"What? What do you mean, related?"

"In Rhode Island, there are two degrees of separation. Everyone I met, in and outside the company, is related to almost everyone else. They are all second cousins, in-laws, and great-great nephews. There's a million people up there, and they all know each other."

"Their advertising is from another century, and their brochures are just as bad. In order to write a meaningful report, I will have to throw some people under the bus. But Joan expects me to be brutally honest."

"Then tell it like it is. You're not shy."

"She wants to see the report before I go back up to present it to the entire senior management team. They're all going to freak out."

CHAPTER 92

Winning Presentation

THREE DAYS after Joan got his report, she called Dave and scheduled his presentation. "Dave, this is great. It's exactly what I need to get these bureaucrats off their butts and take some action. And your monthly fee of fourteen thousand five hundred is fair. I can't wait to see their faces when you make your report. When you come up, our CEO Al wants to meet with you before your presentation."

As soon as Dave arrived at Joan's office, she took him in to meet Al Conover. He jumped up and shook Dave's hand, congratulating him on his excellent proposal. "I read this, and you didn't hold back but told it like it is. I appreciate that kind of candor."

"What's the point of sugarcoating a problem this bad? We've got to turn the company around and fast."

"Yes, we do. And I like your pronoun usage. Come back into my office after the presentation. We can talk some more."

Dave stood at the front of the huge conference room and addressed the thirty or more members of the Executive Management Team seated around the large oval table. As he presented, he looked around trying to determine which man in the group was the marketing VP, whom he hadn't managed to meet on his previous trip. He was about to report some unkind observations of him, but everyone in the room looked nervous. He felt like he was the calmest person there, except for Conover.

The CEO sat in the back corner of the room, away from the huge conference table, and smoked a cigarette. The CEO of a health insurance company smoking in a room full of executives jolted Dave. When Conover caught Dave's eye, he winked and smiled, giving him a thumbs up.

Dave's presentation ended with a sincere round of applause. As the meeting broke up, several executives came up to him and congratulated him. A few others, who he had interviewed on his previous trip, commented that his presentation was excellent.

Back in Conover's office, Dave was greeted by the CEO, Joan, and the one other executive vice president, Dick Nichols.

"I think the fee for the consulting work is expensive," Nichols said.

Dave was prepared for the criticism. "When I was here last, I was privy to proposals of other consultants, including some for your division. By comparison, my rates are about half of any of the others."

Taken aback, Nichols said, "Well, that may be, but they received national recognition and have an impressive track record."

"Well, if that were true, then you wouldn't be in the situation you find yourself. And I also have an enviable track record. I could provide you documentation on vast increases in revenue from national campaigns I created."

Stymied and hesitating, Nichols changed topics and said, "You will be managing a substantial budget as part of your fee. We expect you to spend that money like it's your own."

Astounded by the naivety of the statement, Dave answered. "Mr. Nichols, I always spend my client's money as if it were mine. We are very judicious. It's just the way we do business."

At that point, Conover asked the others to leave so he could have a private conversation with Dave.

"Dave, you had full command in that room, and my staff was prepared to do anything you said. I respect that kind of leadership."

"Thank you. I'm very relaxed when I speak in public. This enables people to let their guard down and actually listen to what I'm saying. And I speak with the confidence of knowing my subject."

"Yes, and there isn't much of that around here. A few minutes ago, you put Dick in his place without insulting him. If we're to succeed, I need more people like you."

"I'm ready to start this assignment immediately."

"Dave, I'm not talking about a consulting project. We will start off with your contract. But I want to put you on my staff as a full-time executive, not a part-time advisor."

"But you can't afford me. I have a successful marketing agency. With the perks of ownership, I probably make more money than Dick Nichols. It just couldn't work."

"We'll find a way. An executive position here is about much more than the money. I want you to go home and think about it. We'll talk again soon."

CHAPTER 93

The Offer and the Invitation

WHEN DAVE GOT HOME, he picked up Elisa and took her to the Saddle River Inn for a special dinner. They celebrated his new consulting contract with RIHIP.

Elisa said, "I was so sure they were going to negotiate the fee down."

"The CEO didn't blink at the cost. But the real problem is that Conover wants me to take a full-time position as VP with the company. I told him he couldn't afford me."

"You're probably right, especially with this huge fee added to our income. But here's something I've been thinking about. As a cancer survivor, I have a pre-existing condition. If I have a recurrence, I may not be able to get health insurance in the future. What would we do then? That would bankrupt us."

"I hadn't thought of that. And you're right, that's a big dark cloud that will hang over us forever."

Joan called Elisa on Saturday morning and told her about Dave's great presentation. She also said Conover called her into his office after Dave left and told her about the job offer. "Elisa, it would be great if you moved here, and Dave took the job."

"We talked about it last night, but Dave is afraid we'd give up too much income. I'm concerned about health insurance in the future."

"I have to tell you. I've been getting a huge fee for my work here, and Conover offered me a full-time position as EVP, Sales & Marketing. The deal is less than my fee, but when you add in all the fringe benefits and perks, I'm coming out way ahead. And the cost of living here is about thirty percent less than the New York area. I'm thrilled with the deal."

"That's great news, Joan. Dave and I will be discussing it further."

"Well, I've been authorized to invite you up next weekend to tour the city and some other attractions. RIHIP will pick up the hotel, meals, and any entertainment expenses. So, pack your bags. You're going to love it up here."

CHAPTER 94

The Sales Pitch

JOAN WAS A NATURAL entertainer. She thrived on being the perfect host. Friday night they had a sumptuous dinner at one of the legendary Italian restaurants on Federal Hill where they enjoyed a series of small plate dishes beautifully garnished. It gave them the chance to taste a large number of the chef's special entreés from various parts of Italy.

Following dinner, they went to the Providence River Fire. This was a monthly event which featured baskets of wood-burning fires in the middle of the Providence River, with instrumental music playing in the background throughout the downtown area.

On Saturday, Joan took them to Newport for lunch and toured Jamestown and the Narragansett beaches. Joan hosted dinner at Capriccio Restaurant Saturday night and golf at Wannamoisett Country Club on Sunday morning as the guest of Dick Nichols.

At most of the venues, they "coincidently" met people that either worked for RIHIP or were connected to it. Joan's planning and staging were flawless.

After golf, Joan took them for a light lunch before their drive home. She explained that after consulting with the insurer for six months, the EVP position was proving quite lucrative for her. "You could sell your agency and invest the proceeds. You'll also be able to put money in the bank on what you'll make here. There are so many perks available to you.

She outlined the total package that the insurer offered. It contained a huge array of benefits, including a company-paid health insurance, 401K plan with matching funds from the company, a generous retirement package with a large pension after a ten-year vestment period, a company car, travel and entertainment expenses, and much more. The residual benefits were endless.

As they drove home Sunday afternoon, Elisa said, "That was a full-court press. Joan can sell anything. Look at all the places we saw and the people we met. It's almost impossible not to accept their offer."

"You're right. She did a great job promoting the deal. I am no longer dismissing the offer. We need to discuss this and make an informed decision."

"The health insurance still looms large in my mind."

"Here are the considerations. What does the total employment package look like? I'm a decision-making entrepreneur. Could I adjust to working full-time for a burgeoning corporate bureaucracy? I already sense some friction from Dick Nichols.

"What do we do with the agency? Can we sell it? What will you do in Rhode Island to keep active? Can you be happy there? At the end of the day, it will be your decision as much as mine."

"I think it's more yours," Elisa told him.

"Then let's take these steps. I'll start consulting under the contract. It will give me a chance to get comfortable in the organization. We'll spend more weekends there to get to know the people and the culture. Then we'll be better prepared to make the right decision.

"In the meantime, you quietly investigate the sale of the agency," he continued. "It can't be worth much, but it must have some value. Call Edelstein. He's always looking to acquire another agency."

Dave sensed her voice rising an octave. "You are kidding, aren't you?"

Laughing, he said, "Yes, but make some calls. If we decide we want to pull the plug and move, we'll know what to expect."

"Dave, that's a sound plan, so let it percolate while you get into the consulting gig. Looking ahead with you, I never know what to expect. We will always have a great adventure ahead of us. I knew the first time I saw you that you were big-trouble. And you never disappoint!"

A week later, Dave began consulting at RIHIP. Elisa put out the word that they were considering selling the agency, she was flooded with calls. Jeff Tashman, the owner of one of the agencies in New York who had worked with Elisa at DBB called her. He had a huge pharmaceutical client in New Jersey and was planning to open an office there. He drove out the next day, looked at their books and office setup, and told her it was exactly what he was looking for.

When Dave got back, he and Elisa had dinner with Tashman, and he presented an offer they couldn't turn down. He offered an amount that was comparable to what Dave had envisioned, based on the current agency valuation formula. But Tashman sweetened the deal by offering to make a second payment, equaling the base price on the one-year anniversary of the sale, if Elisa would stay on for six months to transfer the accounts to the new agency.

After they got home that night, Dave told her about how delighted Conover was with the changes he made to the marketing communications department. The consulting assignment was shaping up to be a dream job, as everyone was getting involved in turning the company around. The only wrinkle was Dick Nichols. He seems to be jealous of Dave's early success in mobilizing the troops. "The guy is a real narcissist."

Elisa was pleased with Dave's news but was more interested in getting into a discussion about Tashman. "What do you think of his deal? I was taken aback by the offer."

"I was thrilled with what he presented. You stay here for six months and we get double what we expected? We can't do better than that. Let's do it."

Tashman had the contract drawn up the following week. Dave got back Thursday night and Tashman came out on Friday, and they executed the contract.

On Tuesday, back in Rhode Island, Joan called Dave into her office. "You've probably been feeling some friction with Dick Nichols, as he was the same with me when I got here. He's a bit insecure."

"Look, Joan, I can stand up to anybody. This guy wants everything to be his idea, so I'll bounce stuff off him before I implement it, so he thinks he's coming up with all the winning ideas."

"Yes! Do that, and also ask him out to play golf. And don't worry about letting him win. He's a two-handicap golfer, so you won't come close to beating him."

"I'll do that, but you know I feel uncomfortable kissing up to anybody. Why can't he just man up?"

Dave shared this conversation with Elisa when they had their Friday date night. And she told him about her week. "Two accounts are increasing their budget going forward, so we may make even more money when we exit the agency."

On Sunday night, Joan called Dave sounding shaken. "Conover was taken to the hospital today coughing up blood."

"That sounds serious. How will it affect the firm?"

"He's bullet-proof. He'll be back in a week. But it was a scare."

"Don't be so sure. He's not a healthy guy. What happens if something happens? I'm scheduled to start negotiating my contract with him in a couple of weeks. If he's not around, is my future in the hands of Nichols?"

"I'll work it out so you will negotiate with me, and he'll bless it."

Hanging up, Elisa could see the change in Dave's look. She sensed something terrible had occurred. Dave then told her about Conover's hospitalization.

The phone call kept Dave awake that night. Everything was falling into place, but that call was delivering an ominous message that was going to change the landscape.

He couldn't stop thinking about it.

Al Conover's management style is what got me to give up our business and take this job. But reporting to a narcissist like Nichols will be impossible. I know it won't work.

His tossing and turning woke Elisa. She turned to him, annoyed. "What's wrong?"

"I could never report to Nichols. It won't work. And we're already committed."

"Stop it. You survived working for a bitch like me. So, suck it up and get to sleep. You'll find a way to make it fun."

Dave hugged Elisa, put his head on the pillow, and fell asleep with a smile.

SPECIAL THANKS
AND ACKNOWLEDGEMENTS

Being an author is said to be a lonely job. It is borne out by the popular perception of an undernourished person being relegated to a cramped room, vacillating from pounding the keyboard to periods of endless writer's block. The bare walls and the stacks of unread books never seem to provide the elusive solution to a bestselling novel.

My reality is quite different, however. I write every day with mixed results, but I sometimes laugh out loud at the humor and get choked up by some of the drama. Until recently, I have always had an office in the front room of our house looking out onto the activity on the street. It provided endless entertainment along with the welcome distraction from the dozens of raucous kids racing up and down the cul de sac on their bikes, scooters, and inline skates. And my bookcase contains more artifacts and trinkets than books.

But what really sets me apart from many of my contemporaries is my support group called The Flash Mob. The individual encouragement and personal contact from these supporters keep me constantly striving to improve my work. This ever-growing list of people who like to read and like to laugh all have personal contact with me through my newsletter, blog posts, and direct communication. They weigh in on cover designs, book descriptions, promotional material, titles/subtitles, plus much more. They all have fun, and the group keeps growing. I hope to surpass 1,000 Mobsters this year.

Several people in the group made substantial contributions in the development of this novel. Alan Nimmy, Larry Venable, Lucy Svagen,

* To learn more, see next page.

Nick DeSimone, Fred Snyder, and Mary Pat Piersons all weighed in on multiple iterations of the title, as well as direction of the storyline.

Of particular note was the extensive effort of Elaine Sisti whose guidance on the character and scene descriptions, as well as the dialog made a dramatic difference in the final iteration.

I also cannot overlook the work of the Koehler Books team that brought this story to life and has contributed to its successful publication. This group of professionals includes Copy Editor Susan Riley, Cover and Text designer Christine Kettner, VP Executive Editor Joe Coccaro, and President/Publisher John Koehler.

THE FLASH MOB

The brainchild of author, Michael A. Sisti, this is a growing number of hundreds of people including friends, business associates, social contacts, and other avid readers with a diverse age, socio-economic, and educational demographic. The common thread is they all like read and are fascinated by the writing process.

"I don't know of any other author that has organized an advisory group of this size. I never feel like I am trapped in a room, staring at a screen, suffering from writer's block. I simply call in the Mob.
And the best part is, we're all having fun."
—**Michael A. Sisti**

"My firm has published nearly a thousand books for 940 authors, with sales of over 900,000 books. While most authors have a fan base, Michael Sisti has a dedicated organization. Sisti's first book with us is the product of this synergetic collaboration, and why we signed him. We have great expectations that his entire book series will be extremely successful."
—**John Koehler**, President, Koehler Books

FOR MORE INFORMATION:
WWW.MICHAELSISTI.COM/FLASH-MOB

Milton Keynes UK
Ingram Content Group UK Ltd.
UKHW011043201123
432908UK00006BA/1012